CARDINAL NUMBERS

CARDINAL NUMBERS

●

HOB BROUN

ALFRED A. KNOPF ⊠ NEW YORK 1988

"Blood Aspens" and "Rosella, in Stages" were
originally published in *The Quarterly*.

Library of Congress Cataloging-in-Publication Data
Broun, Hob.
Cardinal numbers.
I. Title.
PS3552.R6824C37   1988   813'.54   87-40481
ISBN 0-394-56261-5

Manufactured in the United States of America

FIRST EDITION

A NOTE ON THE TYPE

This book was set on the Linotype in Granjon, a type named
in compliment to Robert Granjon, a type cutter and printer active
in Antwerp, Lyons, Rome, and Paris, from 1523 to 1590.
Linotype Granjon was designed by George W. Jones,
who based his drawings on a face used by Claude Garamond
(c. 1480-1561) in his beautiful French books. Granjon more
closely resembles Garamond's own type than does any of
the various modern faces that bear his name.
Composed by Maryland Linotype Composition Company,
Baltimore, Maryland
Printed and bound by The Haddon Craftsmen, Scranton, Pennsylvania
Designed by Iris Weinstein

FOR WOODIE AND JANE,
ONE MAN'S FAMILY

CONTENTS

●

CARDINAL NUMBERS

ICE WATER

●

E V E N in mid-December, wearing two sweaters, window glass rattling in dead putty there at the back of the shop, Schenck drank only ice water. It rippled on his throat, against the wall of his stomach. It cleared his palate and cleansed his bladder. He drank down a gallon or more in a day, not from an excess of thirst—his appetites were diffident—but vigilantly, to maintain a pattern of comfort and good feeling. Always, Schenck had guarded his habits.

Opening the minifridge balanced on phone directories and accordion files, he took a refill from the pitcher. Pain in his knuckles was best relieved by heat, and yet Schenck had never held a teacup with familiar reassurance as he held this glass. He bent back his head, let ice cubes fall against his teeth, saw the uneven black tin ceiling, and indulged an image of it giving way. Everything would fall around him, but nothing on him. Schenck's safety of place held its own in the impacted city, amid all its reprisals.

Some lugubrious piano piece came over WNYC as he stood with his feet under the radiator by the display window and read a letter from a client in New Haven asking that he locate a particular translation of Heine. As a student in Vienna just after the war, Schenck had been inspired by the early lyrics, even memorizing parts of the Nordsee cycles. Storm-whipped waves and glistening crags. Schenck's ambition then had been for the stage, to secrete himself inside the great roles. Iago, Cyrano, Faust. All sorts of peaks had been foreseeable then, a tame, benign delusion in which, no doubt, there was less sin than in the pride he now took in the humility of old age.

Buzzing of the security-wired door startled him badly. A tousled woman in high boots and a man's raglan overcoat came at him.

"I need something for a girl eleven. Very bright. Loves animals."

Her smile was ferocious.

"Pictures? Something with pictures?"

"That's not necessarily what I meant." The woman gestured curiously in front of her mouth as though drawing out a tapeworm and winding it on a stick. "She reads novels all by herself. Jack London. Dickens. Really quite exceptionally mature, I think."

Schenck managed to sell her the memoirs of a ninteenth-century Irish veterinarian—hand-tinted engravings and marbled endpapers, twenty-five bucks. And then she asked him to wrap it.

"This is a department store? You see gift paper here? You want wrapping, go down two blocks to Wexel's and buy some."

———

S C H E N C K dined alone, by candlelight, on smoked fish and macaroni salad. He ate too quickly, afterwards slowly drank his ice water, detecting synthetic undertones probably traceable to a plastic ice tray, which he now dropped in the garbage. No more of those.

The apartment over the shop, a series of low rooms off a long L-shaped passage, was too large for him. Three of these rooms he used only for storage. They were clogged with furniture and crates of books, armoires, washstands, a Peruvian hammock, brass lamps, Hogarth reproductions, a library bought blind three years ago from an executor in Mount Kisco and never looked through. And his bedroom, in the shorter leg of the L, was divided by folding screens, the half-space less shadowy, more settled.

And one room was empty except for the director's chair in which he waited now by the window that gave onto the air shaft. He waited in the dark until past eleven—later than usual—when the light came on across the way as two opposing V's projected from top and bottom of the lampshade onto the beige wall. Sheila came naked to the window and put her hands on the glass. She could look straight at him and still seem not to see. Graying hair was undone; breasts hung almost to her navel. She would stand there for five or ten minutes, swaying, expressionless, and then disappear.

This is a very long quarrel, he thought. I am not competent to judge.

Schenck had claim to a small period of marriage, and while he worked at resistance, this ritual at the windows inevitably stirred random memories of that time. He had been forty, newly a citizen, employed in a machine shop owned by Czechs. Penny was an obstreperous girl, and large. She had been raised on a dairy farm and referred to all other women as "heifers." They were married somewhere in New Jersey with two strangers from a luncheonette as witnesses. Penny ate red meat at every meal, and liked to make love standing up. She couldn't learn to drive but played competent chess. At the end of their third summer she left for a day at Rockaway Beach and never came back. In 1971 she mailed him divorce papers from Elko, Nevada, where she and the man she'd met on the subway were managing a ten-unit motel.

All that Schenck knew for certain about Sheila was her name. Data solicited in the neighborhood were conflicting: She was shy and retiring, snooty and arrogant, a high-average bowler, known to keep odd hours, deeply religious, a "cocktail waitress," a divorcee from California. The informants all spoke with an unexampled lack of vehemence, as though describing a fictional character. Schenck had not decided anything, but as an adjective for her attraction he most often took up "opaque." That seemed fair. Standing naked at her window, she was completely opaque.

———

B Y closing time on Friday, Schenck had written in his ledger these sales:

Wallace, Alfred Russell   *The Maylay Archipelago* $10 –
    (boards slightly foxed)
de Assis, Machado   *Philosopher or Dog?*   8.50
Pynchon, Thomas   *Crying of Lot Forty-nine*   35 –
    (1st edition w/ wrapper)

Day total: $53.50
           4.28 (tax)
Week total: $457.73
Year total: $28,693.19
Week avg. $562.62

At six-thirty, earlier than usual, Ugo tapped on the window. He held up a white parcel, gestured with his eyes.

"I was just about to go up," Schenck said, now reengaging the locks.

Ugo stamped and blew and tugged at the ends of his long red muffler. He crackled the deli paper. "Lombardese braciola. Filet of beef cured in salt and then air-dried. It's a little like prosciutto, only milder."

Ugo had begun as a garrulous loiterer in the shop during breaks from rehearsal of an off-off production of Pirandello's *Right You Are (If You Think So)*; transforming himself from a nuisance into a friend had taken a year. Schenck's spiny reticence made him unavailable to all but the truly persistent. And still Ugo needed to certify every visit with a gift. These had lately become more elaborate, and Ugo wore the slight, perpetual smile of a dolphin or a beluga whale. All by himself, without an agent, he'd bagged a gangster part, three months guaranteed, on the daytime serial, *Edge of Night*.

Easily annoyed but hard to embarrass, Schenck was both when presented with a dressing gown from Lord & Taylor.

Ugo said: "This is my first TV job with lines since I did an anti-Semitic janitor on *The Defenders* in 1962. Why shouldn't we both enjoy it?"

And this was the Ugo who once had said that he yearned for subtleties but was trapped in a culture of noise.

They ate the braciola with capers and olive oil, finished with a romaine salad. Schenck poured Chartreuse for Ugo, ice water for himself, and they torpidly resumed their ongoing game of casino. Score: 18,201 to 18,169, Schenck leading. Ugo, naturally, saw this parity as a signal, if not a proof, of their fellowship, but Schenck called the game defective since luck determined what skill should have.

"It's like a coin-flip experiment," he said, sweeping in the ten of diamonds. "All that's decided is that you can't decide."

Schenck, gazing at his friend, at Ugo's clumsy fan of cards, the tufts sheep-white around his bullet head, his waxy eyes and incomprehensible tics, felt dismay. And in his effacement of clothes, the shabby poplin zip jacket, cuffs and collar frayed like a busboy's, the welfare pants he could scale fish in, there was something willfully craven and dreadful. So much did he resemble the bumbler who onstage would not know what to do with his hands—was it conceivable at all that he'd been in Actors' Equity for almost thirty years?

But in another moment, one flourish of liqueur, he was singing "When Yuba Plays the Tuba Down in Cuba" in an elegant tennis-club drawl, with soft shoes, and then, in the space of a spin, hitting every note of defiance in "Was I Drunk, Was He Handsome, and Did My Ma Give Me Hell?"

Schenck whistled appreciation. "Ugo, you should go on stage."

Clammy and pale, Ugo lipped the Chartreuse bottle, groping for any chair. "All the hells of Dante," he said vaguely.

———

S C H E N C K rose earlier than usual on Christmas Day, which was not white. He went downstairs to the shop and retrieved the *Times* from in front of the door. Back in bed, vivified by two full tumblers, leafing quickly toward the crossword, he found this among the death notices on page 18:

GLASSER—Jean-Pierre. Beloved husband of Ciel, loving father of Todd, Mimi, and Sara, dear brother of Simone Taubman, adored uncle of Mario, cherished cousin, devoted godfather, and friend to many. Pre-deceased by parents Bernard and Rosa Glasser of Deerfield Beach, FL. His warmth and generosity of spirit touched all who knew him. A proud fighter, he died as he had lived, with passion. Memorials will be appreciated to the Topaze Research Foundation, or American Ballet Theatre.

In 1969, Jean-Pierre Glasser had put up money enabling Schenck to open the bookshop, at that point stocked mainly with Schenck's personal collection. Devoted godfather, and friend to many. They had met by chance in the lobby of the Carnegie Hall Cinema, at a showing of Von Sternberg's *The Blue Angel*. Schenck admitted reading the subtitles, that his native German had been distant, indistinct, a passing wind. Harmony of émigrés! (Glasser was a Jew from Quebec.) They had dinner that night and enthused over Dietrich the humiliator. In this phase, Schenck was looking around for an ally.

He studied the ice cube remnants in a puddle at the bottom of the tumbler. They were opaque now, not glassy as before, and shaped like charcoal briquettes. He recalled his discovery of baseball that '69 summer, wearing a Mets cap everywhere: impenetrable laws of assimilation. And that vivid afternoon in the new shop—which people stumbled quickly in and out of as though it were an occupied toilet—when he reached his ice water epiphany during the listless late-Sunday innings of a televised doubleheader, that first experience of calm, silvery perfection from tongue to glottis to gut.

Schenck completed the puzzle, except for an unfair corner where "Spiny shrub" was crossed with "Former 5-franc coin in Brussels." The clock read nine-fifteen, and he could not think of anything to do.

——

o n Wednesday he waited for Sheila until 2 a.m., but her light never came on. Could she have relatives to visit? He felt lower than he had the night before, alone with bad news then, and without a single clear remembrance of Christmas childhood, the sweet sadness of which might have been balm. The deficit was not of his memory, but of the past itself, which was evidently tainted with self-erasure, a slow rot working from the inside out.

He was aground in the present, dreaming of Sheila nearly all the time now. In these dreams she was always severely clothed, like a governess, rigorous and strict in her speech and behavior. So he was afraid to sleep, late as it was, afraid not of the dreaming but of waking into the naked fact of her absence from the window. He stayed up all night reading James's *Transatlantic Sketches*, drinking his water.

And he did not open the shop on Thursday, but instead hiked uptown to the park, shivered on a bench near Belvedere Castle. There were blowing papers, decrepit pigeons, and a smoky, tenuous sky to complete the scene. Schenck's appearance might have been one of pathos or absurdity or fecklessness or withdrawal, any and all; or within lines firm and definitive, he might be the emblem of aging, a painter's subject (or object) with brown, oatmeal-grain coat against green bench slats, a messily furled umbrella resting across his knees.

Gloveless, his hands twinged and tingled so badly that they could not stand the pressure of his pockets. He hurried down Madison Avenue, losing the race with nightfall. Already there were happy drunks, and surly drunks, and to complete the scene, store windows dressed with plush reindeer and cotton snow.

Blue exhaust clouded in his way led to a mental picture: Sheila coming back to the city on a bus, coming away from a company town in western Pennsylvania, from the diligent miseries of her visit. Schenck's rarely exercised imagination frisked with detail: the artificial tree, the wreath of painted pine cones, Father pouring rum from a holiday decanter, kidding unpleasantly; diabetic Auntie with her blotched face and white fur slippers; icicles cracking off the eaves outside; her now unfamiliar bedroom with a fresh box of Kleenex and a clock that ticked too loudly; and finally, knees together, handbag grasped to her stomach, there on the bus reviewing the variations of her life, indifference and cruelty, chords and arpeggios.

——

ON Friday, when he came to open up, a man was waiting at the door, a junkie with a carton of worthless paperbacks. Schenck gave him ten bucks, realizing they'd all come now, and thinking: Let them. It had just begun to snow, lightly, in dry, tufted flakes that were easily blown.

He looked through his shelves, at a tissue fold-out map from an Alpine geography, at photographs of Bedouin herders, Alban Berg, a Kyoto hotel; at the ludicrous jacket copy of a Baroness Orczy romance, and recognized the absence of a coziness that should by rights have been there, inside the steamy heat with snow feathering against the windows, among his books and books and books in their hammer-dented, varnish-wanting shelves.

He closed at noon, no sales recorded, and went to the Hellas for lunch. There, beside the steam table, like Italians in a barbershop, the brothers had taped postcards of home, a scenic hill town overlooking the Aegean. Outside, the snow was building. There was no wind. Schenck thought: All my insurance is up to date. The meat loaf was dry, and needed extra gravy; the green beans spurted warm water when bitten.

Morning came dry and crisp and gray. Schenck ironed his corduroy jacket, shaved carefully. His hat was tight, both hands throbbed, but the arrangement of smudges on white wall seemed lovely, undifficult. He went slowly, like someone his age, planting both feet on a step before the next move down. At the empty street he paused for minutes. Children stared, and he turned the corner, thinking of all that had not proved inexpressible across an air shaft. There was her name on the bell board. The bridge swayed. He decided to flip a coin.

B Y T H E N U M B E R S

●

[1]

They worked at the enclosed mall in King of Prussia. They wore plastic nametags, the corporate logo above a deep groove accommodating a Dymo label. Jenelle for the record store, Courtney for the bookstore. They had received reprimands for lateness.

[2]

Dinner is interesting. The plastic bag doesn't melt in the boiling water. You cut off the top with scissors and lobster Newburg comes out.

From the paper: "Dartmouth Warnell, 19, of North Philadelphia, while attempting to escape from police custody, was shot and killed in the parking lot of the Afro-American Cultural Museum. A warrant for driving-while-suspended had been outstanding."

The table is a phone company cable spool which occasionally insinuates a splinter. The VCR format is unchic: Beta. The movie from the rental store traces an anchorwoman who finally turns into a werewolf on the air. They've seen it before.

[3]

Saturdays there are special events at the mall. It could be a ho-ho banjo band in red vests and sleeve garters. Or a begonia club. Or a cat show. There might be Cub Scouts all over the place. Everyone seems to put in the extra effort on a Saturday. Their jaws ache from smiling.

[4]

Courtney and Jenelle together in a bath. Pubic hair is ugly, but they're afraid to shave. Many products for the hair, each based on a wholesome foodstuff. Plastic bottles bobbing.

J: I wish my toes were long and thin like yours.

[4A]

Courtney and Jenelle in a stall shower, embracing in soap foam. Why they're late all the time. Mist.

[4B]

Courtney and Jenelle washing clothes by the Orinoco. (Black-and-white, dubbed.)

C: Why can't I get my skirts as bright as yours?

J: You're not beating them hard enough.

Rising smoke in the distance, music of chain saws.

[5]

She had enough imagination to feel molten plastic when she took the albums from the carton. These were red mostly, with lettering in white. There was a song about land reform, another about mascara. She thought of wearing leather next to the skin.

"Where would I find language instruction tapes?"

She shelved the travel guides in overstock, felt once more this alien regret at not being able to type. Letters to show the way. Orange signs in her sightline: Romance Cooking Health & Fitness. She thought about her eyes in someone else's face on posters all over town.

"Do you have *How to Avoid Probate*?"

[6]

Jenelle's mother lives by herself in Cherry Hill in a house that's almost paid for. Dad is trying to make a cleaning service go in south Alabama; he calls often, seems not to be doing well. She has brown hair, type O blood, allergies to shellfish and aluminum foil.

Courtney's mother is Japanese, a war bride. Her father died last summer of asbestosis. Her brother is in his third year of biochemistry at Drexel. She is right-handed, underweight, wears glasses to correct a mild astigmatism.

[7]

They could be married to men like sleds on rails: top ten percent of the class, membership in a rowing club, an ability to anticipate currency fluctuations. They could be plain in Quaker bonnets, humming as they card wool, shaded sweetly by belief.

[7A]

Rod turned back to her in his belted leather coat of a too-shiny material that was not leather. His wide dark eyes glistened with forgiveness. Courtney inhaled the coat's laboratory musk as he gathered her up in his arms.

[7B]

Jenelle heard the whispers in passing, her gray skirts brushing the cobbles, the black book cradled in her hand. She had broken the silence in fear, but her quiet simple words had then seemed to lift all eyes in the meetinghouse.

[8]

Was it a party? Jenelle is lying in bed, cold cucumber slices balanced on her face. She has unplugged the stereo, forbidden music. Wondering if he really will phone tonight, Courtney wishes for an interesting birthmark. Someone downstairs is raking leaves. Jenelle has an enema and feels better.

J: Why don't we have towels that match? With our initials intertwined in a contrasting color?

C: I don't know.

[o]

Strollers were unconsciously arranged around the fountain; the mothers could not wake their children. Earring Emporium had not had a customer all day. An NCR repairman set down his tool kit and wandered aimlessly. The sound track was muddy for Cinema III's matinee. A man with no family bought a badminton set and charged it. An aquarium burst spontaneously at Petsateria; there was a brief waterfall over jagged glass, and then little flips on the carpet. . . .

Courtney took the taped package out from behind the stockroom fire extinguisher. Her mouth was dry. The package felt funny. Too heavy? Too light? She was late for the rendezvous. . . .

Jenelle put the mustard on her pretzel left-to-right, signing everything was go. Slowly, as if browsing, they moved toward the Westgate exit, past Jeans World, Muffy's, the Cookie Castle. They were being followed. The two men wore state trooper glasses and trim black chin beards, but weren't as young as they thought. Were they DEA? Libyans? No hesitation. Jenelle took the silver gun from under her rabbit jacket and gave each one two in the face. JFK time, brains on a pink dress. . . .

Courtney and Jenelle hydroplaning in a white Camaro, spinning across three lanes of expressway, coming out of it and going harder on. The windshield a gray boil. Hiss of the police-band radio. Swerving headlights. The needle edging past 100. . . .

"Don't you read?" Courtney said.

"No, I've finished school."

"Read and you'd know nothing ever happens to us. Just these little vignettes we're not even aware of."

"You mean it?"

"Anyway *they* do."

"Okay."

Jenelle threw the package out the window, bit off the tip of the silver barrel. The gun was made of wax and contained a thin lime syrup.

[—1]

Courtney and Jenelle in a cemetery with hoagies. From this elevation it is possible to see a white church, the empty river. New shoots of grass are just starting. The air is soft, receptive to the least aroma trace. Starlings forage between grave aisles, behind bronze-doored crypts. Oil trickles over Courtney's lip. Jenelle catches it on her finger.

C: I wish we were in our eighties and could look back.
J: Me too.

[oo]

What then do we want words for?

The tab on a file.

To say this was in Pennsylvania, during the second term of Reagan.

B L O O D A S P E N S

●

TH E outlaw camp was on the middle fork of the Flathead between Horseshoe Peak and the Divide. Ponies nodded over their
hay in the corral and jaybirds called from out of the big pines.
Inside the loghouse, Buzz (Dan Duryea) was feeding the stove
from a basket of cobs to heat a kettle of red beans and jerky.
The wall behind him was hung with snakeskins and calendar
art. He couldn't remember the name of the song he was humming and by now he'd stopped trying. He spat on the stove and
it hissed.

Wiley (Andy Devine) came in from the dooryard and
went to rummage in his medicine box. They called him "El
Paciente" because he never stopped whining about his ailments.
Lumbago today and bursitis tomorrow or palsy or milk leg or
grippe. He brought over his packets of herbs and put a pan of
water on the stove to make tea.

Wiley said: "Smells good."

Buzz snorted. "Jerky and beans. Like always."

Wiley said: "Put in plently of chili pods. It cleans out
your system."

Buzz said: "I like mine to stay dirty."

Out by the hayrick, Midnight (Marlon Brando) was planting geranium slips in a rusted-through pump trough. One night he'd lost three fingers blowing a safe, but he was still deft anytime he worked with his hands. His long lank black hair fell down the back of his buckskin shirt. His boots glistened with mink oil. Midnight had an Oglala wife somewhere and two boys, but it'd been years since he left.

Jackdaws were squawking in the dusk. Hard rain began to fall as Costain (Rod Taylor) came down off the ridge in his linen duster, four cutthroat trout in his bag. A wide Stetson brim darkened features that were already nut brown and fixed in their usual blank expression. They called him "High Wide and Handsome." He opened the loghouse door and saw the stable hand naked on the end bunk. He had Wiley's cock in his mouth and Midnight was greasing his butt with lard.

Buzz said: "Juanito got drunk on liniment again and he's ready for love."

Costain's granddaddy had ridden with Quantrill's raiders. Costain lit a cigarillo and . . .

(two pages missing)

. . . so Wiley and Midnight took the weasels down to the river edge for skinning. The water ran heavy with spring melt and the beach was halved. They scrubbed their knives with sand and it soaked up the blood. They pegged out the pelts to dry and threw the meat in the water because Wiley said these weasels and stoats and martens and so on carried disease like the rats in Europe.

Wiley said: "Plague." He nodded in that way that meant he'd studied up on whatever he was saying.

Midnight said: "We better wash our hands real good then."

The stink of copper smelters down the valley came on the freshening wind. Costain knew it was 1910. People were starting to laugh at just the idea of road agents.

Buzz kicked out at the barbed-wire fence. He said: "These Basque bastards and their sheep."

But Costain knew better.

He said: "Perreault ain't no Basque. He's a general from France. Got drummed out of the Foreign Legion. Married a rich girl in Boston. Her father give him the ranch so's he'd go away."

Buzz said: "Fuck him anyway," and took out his wire cutters.

Town was asleep at that time of day. There was only one horse tied to the railing in front of the pharmacy. The green mortar-and-pestle sign squeaked on its hinges. Costain and Buzz put on bear masks made out of paper. They busted the glass out of the door on their way in. Buzz swung on an old farmer who reached inside his black coat.

Costain warned him: "Watch my .38," but the old man kept reaching and Costain spun him with one shot and put a hole through his neck. The outlaw pair took four hundred in gold and paper and a brass-bound chest full of cocaine syrup and ether and belladonna and sleeping powders. A boy ran up in the street outside and Buzz gut-shot him.

Buzz said: "Mask slipped. He saw my face."

The boy went into convulsions in the dirt. Red foam came to his mouth.

Costain said: "Finish him."

The cut load took the boy's skull apart and Buzz wiped brain off his boots. Then they rode hard up the draw and crossed the Flathead at the first show of treeline. Costain swept their trail with pine boughs. Then they cut north through the shallows . . .

(remainder of page mutilated)

. . . and threw his cards down.

Midnight said: "Plainly it ain't or I wouldn't be asking."

Wiley said: "Don't you read three queens?"

The stove had gone out and night frost come up on the windows, but they paid no mind. Costain was rattling coins in his hand. Midnight was pawing at an empty syrup bottle. His face was all puffed up and had confusion in it.

Buzz said: "Should of seed it. First slug puts him in rotation like a top. Then High Wide gives him the cup of grass on the next one and near takes his head off clean."

Midnight said: "Shut up and deal."

Wiley had his eyes open like a trance, but he was snoring. The loghouse smelled of blankets. The wick of the lamp was turned low. Costain brought the bandanna soaked in ether up to his face.

Buzz said: "Fuck cards."

Oil dripped off the edge of Midnight's whetstone. Bits of steel shaved from the blade were too small to see. Midnight was nodding to the rhythm of scrapes. Hair fell over his eyes.

He said: "How 'bout I cut you a new asshole?"

Buzz shot out of his chair and flapped his hand over an empty holster. A fist came down hard on the table and it was Costain's.

He said: "Quit now. Stow it before I have to lay both of you out."

The rivals stared at each other a long minute and the heat came into their eyes.

Costain said: "Midnight. Get some air. Go find Juanito."

It was so fresh outside. Midnight stood under the moon clear as water and threw up his arms. Trees and fenceposts made long shadows and his breath made steam. The stars seemed to flare. A chicken ran out from under the porch. Midnight caught her up and opened her throat on the blade. He sucked blood from his finger stumps.

In the morning Juanito was missing with two horses. Each man went alone to his cache and found it untouched. Then they looked for a trail sign. They walked in mist to their knees and a silence that was tense. Costain had been expecting something but not exactly this. He knew there was a supply of time being used up and nothing he could do about that.

To himself Wiley said: "We got to take steps."

He was thinking how it would be sad to leave this place, where Juanito was sure to bring law on purpose or by accident. He liked being near water. He liked being right under the sky. Anywhere else would bring on his claustrophobia.

The search was called off at noon. Midnight stayed behind in the woods to drink cocaine syrup and curse the others. In the loghouse, Costain got out his maps.

Buzz said: "What the hell are you so calm about?"

Costain did not look up.

Buzz said: "Let's just torch the place and ride."

Wiley was stroking his pelt bundles. He said: "We made this. We worked it up and around and . . ."

Costain told them both to shut up. His eyes narrowed. He

said: "Three will take a week's provisions and head out for the Beaverhead. The other one will find Juanito and quiet him."

Wiley said: "Can we go to the hot springs on the way?"

The deck of cards came out and Wiley volunteered to sit for Midnight.

Costain cut himself a red four. He said: "Low card wins. I'll go."

They agreed to meet at the needle rocks on the first day of May and swore a pact of blood to die free. Buzz had tears in his eyes. Midnight had to be clubbed to stop his raving and then tied to his pinto. They took off just at dusk and followed a feeder creek up across the ridge. Further on they found a cave dug out of the red rock that would conceal their fire. They made camp and Buzz and Wiley lit into one another over who should've put coffee on the packhorse and hadn't.

Buzz said: "But for that greaser punk, we wouldn't be asquat down in mud with fried biscuit for dinner."

Midnight said: "You gone soft?"

They laid themselves down, but nobody slept. There was bat stink in the cave and a cold seep that had them all rucked up in their blankets.

——

COSTAIN knew how to be careful. He wore a false mustache and ordered rye whiskey with a Spanish accent. The pianola was playing "Strawberry Blonde." The mine drudgers had already shed their pay, so all the tables were empty except the one where Perreault could be seen. He had a cigar in his mouth and his finger up the girl child on his lap. Costain would have got him outside and hijacked his pockets but for the business at hand.

He said to the barman: "Seen my cousin tonight? He berry thin witha long hair."

The answer came: "Yah, I seen ten guys like that and I didn't ask nobody's name."

This barman was a safecracker lammed from Cleveland first and then Denver. Talking the hour with Costain, he could boil it down and see they were comrades.

He said: "Want help with this Mex pigeon a yers, then I could be the man."

Costain hadn't dropped his guard for nothing. He could recognize an asset when it came up, and this one had a kind of city smarts that would fit.

Costain said: "Meet me on the back street with a bottle."

———

T H E drizzle lasted all morning. Wiley's horse came up lame and had to be walked. They pulled up where aspens were in bud and scrounged for dry wood, but the fire was more steam than smoke. Midnight's feet were swole up, so he couldn't get his boots off.

Buzz thumbed Costain's hand-drafted map and said: "Settler's cabin marked right two mile off. I say we go down and get proper fed. See what else might look good while we're in the neighborhood."

Wiley said: "You go on. My gut burns fit to kill."

That knife went clean through wet leather. Midnight had it figured to the minute. He was going to walk the mountain on bloody feet till he found the Virgin Mary and got clean.

Chicago said he knew about a Mex hideout in Bilby and why didn't they go over there. The sun was going thump inside Costain's hangover and all he could do was grunt. They rode four miles down the wagon-road ruts, but it was slow going in the mud and Chicago was impatient for a shortcut. Costain stopped to light a cigarillo.

Chicago blew rain off his lips and whispered: "Thing of it is you told me all I need to know last night."

And then he brought up the Derringer and shot Costain through the eye. He stripped the body and hobbled the horse. He cut out for the Flathead camp with Costain's ears tied to his belt and bouncing.

(here ends recovered manuscript)

IS THIS

CIVILIZATION?

●

AMERICAN architecture is what you can see from the road. That's what I tell my class, and they put it down in their notebooks. The stout girl in the front row (I think her name is Bonnie) looks pointedly at her watch. She is dutiful, like all my students, but not interested in much. I think: This isn't what I had in mind, either. I dismiss them ten minutes early and sit in the quiet room watching it snow.

My apartment is chilly, the furnace clacking down below. I place my new space heater by the tub and soak a long time. The nightgown I put on has been washed so often the piping has come loose from around the collar. I take out some cold lentils, dress them with olive oil and what can be squeezed from a hard old lemon half, listen to a Dave Clark Five album, the oldest in my collection. On the back cover, under a leafy bower of red ballpoint ink, are my initials, S.E.A. Later, I get in bed to read, but my head tows me under. I fall asleep with all the lights on, the book cradled in my arm like a doll.

———

BARBARA intercepts me outside the library. She is giving a dinner party for "interesting women," and wants me to attend. An NPR reporter will be there, a peace activist visiting from Israel, two illustrators, an oncologist, and Sue Willens from the Drama Department. Barbara glitters with enthusiasm, or it could just be snow settling on her lashes. I don't think much of an obligation to be interesting, but say I'll call her by the weekend.

Someone has to do the freshman lit. surveys, and it's Barbara. Possibly having been raised on a farm with eight brothers is useful in this respect. She speaks constantly of her family, of her writing hardly ever, which is how I can tell she's serious about it.

Though it's completely out of sequence, I spend today's class on Louis Sullivan. We look at details of the Carson Pirie Scott store, foliage intricately incised above the doorways. I show slides of Sullivan's small-town Minnesota banks, slides Corey and I took one summer. Mistakenly among them is one he must have snapped without my knowing. In workshirt and white slacks, I kneel by a picnic table and stare at my hand. My expression is one of dismay, as if something were painfully embedded there. The sun is low behind me. I am unsettled by the picture, unable to recall ever having seen it before.

I take the long way home, two legs of a triangle. Ice lumps turn in the slow porridge of the river. Long mill buildings, low storage lockers, seem solid and husklike at once. In a livelier, more solvent city, I realize, all this would be reclaimed, the brick blasted clean and a design center or galleria installed. Much prettier this way, dead.

———

M Y office is small to begin with, and on top of that, I double up. Alice has been teaching here for nearly thirty years, and she is very particular. I would say fussy, but her unrelenting dignity precludes it. Clear pushpins only are allowed on the cork board we share and I must stand in the hall to smoke. But Alice has given me the desk by the window because, she says, "You're pale as shortening."

Guiltily, I am clearing away a month's unopened mail. Outside, while turning everything to mush, the sun resembles something membranous and insubstantial. I scrabble through drawers for a cigarette, decide to chew a rubber band instead. There is a card from Holly, my brightest student of two years ago; on its front, a woodcut of mountains, and under that, "La poesía es como el pan, para todos."

Inside there is this:

> This will need to be in a hurry because I have a tutorial in forty minutes. This town, like you said, is full of noise, but I'm getting along. I have a room near campus in a house with turret gables and I'm seeing a man who makes sailboats, which is okay though he's not very physical. We might go down to Baja this summer. Nothing much to say, except when I do something I want it to be the way you would.
>
> I really love you,
> Holly

Bright but backward, much too old to have a crush on her teacher. Or possibly I'm misled by embarrassment, lured into evasion. Might this be a defect of the "interesting woman"? I drop the card in my bag, knowing I won't write back.

I catch a chill at Thriftway just from shuffling through the frozen entrees. Indecision is always dangerous. So I stick firmly to inedibles: a set of jumper cables, wood glue, mouthwash, aluminum-foil loaf pans, a plastic helicopter, *Self* magazine. In the checkout line, watching a short, placid man watching me, I realize the rubber band is still in my mouth.

⸺

ɪ ᴛ ' s Friday and I go to see Corey. The temperature has sharply dropped, turning yesterday's slush into mean ice troughs, making the drive difficult. But I never miss a Friday. I sway and spin up into the hills, past long black driveways and houses built, in a simpler period, to be above the soot.

Corey's father comes out across the porch and puts his arms around me. He's all overbearing bone at first, then something gives inside and it seems the only thing holding him up is his chin hooked over my shoulder.

"Everything smooth?" I ask.

"Tolerable."

He takes my gloves, tugs at my coat, but I won't let him have it.

"I don't warm up till April."

He smooths his mustache, which is yellowing like ivory. "Go on ahead. He's heard the door." His eyes ascend so slowly, as if counting each carpeted stair.

Corey's room overlooks the back garden, but the spot he prefers for his chair is away from the window, under a wedge of white ceiling where the roof slants around a dormer. He pretends to be surprised.

"Na aun. Aun!"

I lift the bill of his Pirates cap, tickle his lashes with mine.

"Loom spox," he whispers slyly.

The damage came not from the accident but from surgery afterward, a futile try to reattach his right arm, severed by the guardrail. An anesthetist's blunder, loss of oxygen to the brain, permanence. Corey's father might have sued, but the blunt mechanics of the process made him turn away.

"I've made a lot of money, some of it in not very pleasant ways," he said. "But, goddamn, I won't squeeze my boy like he is for profit."

Corey can walk just fine, even dance, but he'd rather sit, his one arm gone above the elbow, the other one withered, useless mostly, nerves crushed when his Kawasaki came back down out of the air.

"Potos," he says, nodding at the chocolate apple as I break it into sections. "Owow potos."

It's hard to know how much he remembers or now understands. The doctor says to think of it like a stroke, certain sectors of the brain cut off. But which ones? I think Corey cries at magazines because he can't take pictures anymore, but I'm not sure. He adores music sometimes, or it can send him into a rage. Sometimes he'll turn his back to me if I speak, but not today. I feed him chocolate in small bits to make it last and describe a John Garfield movie, the new prison going up at the north end of Rock City Road, about Barbara's party and why I don't want to go. Quizzically, he watches my lips. And, as always, when I take him out of his pants, he's all ready. What I always say: This is something he can't do for himself. But, of course, it's at least as much for me, a small stolen serenity, all his veins and capillaries. And so I think of the big

house over us, of joists and beams and lath. Corey looks gravely
at what he has put in my hand. I make a fist around it, stand
at the window. Catbirds swoop to millet in the feeder. There
is a jagged trench in the snow where Corey's father has
shoveled, thrown salt, given up.

—

T O D A Y the sun is bright and kids are playing hockey in the
street. I spend an hour putting on toenail polish, as if planning
to appear somewhere in sandals. Barbara calls, very tense about
her party. I turn up the radio, pretending someone else is here,
promise to call back later. Then I make a pot of gunpowder
tea and, as though back in high school, write down this dream
I had.

A white-trashy house where I'm staying in Los Angeles,
old TV sets in the yard and an avocado tree no one ever picks
from. A big screen porch with everybody sitting on car seats,
or the floor, men with ponytails and marijuana-leaf belt
buckles. Woman in underwear with runny nose, two others
passing a can of mushroom soup, spoon sticking out. Can't
understand how these people have three Hindu servants (father,
two small sons in bellboy suits). Disparaging remarks made to
and about servants. Laughter. Very nasty. I say to frog-faced
man, "You should keep your fucking mouth shut," start to
leave. "Is this civilization?" he asks. I say, very righteous, "No,
just decency." Then walking past motel where there's been
some disturbance, street littered with broken glass: green,
milky, clear, ribbed, frosted. Nature of perception. Real pos-
sibilities. Walk on to unkempt park, eucalyptus leaves on
ground, newspapers in lake. Police everywhere. A child has

been murdered, they need a culprit and I'm handy. Hemmed in with questions, knocked down. They're kicking me. Black jackets, yelling. Then Corey pushes in to the rescue, but they grab his hair and it comes off. His head is all white. Running in the water to escape is when I wake up.

Barbara calls a little after four, very upset. The artichoke bisque has scorched. The illustrators have quarreled and aren't coming. Okay, okay. The minute I hang up, I realize the only thing I have to wear that's interesting needs to be cleaned.

I'm the last one there, the only one wearing a dress, and Barbara seems mad. I say how nice everything looks, and what are these called?

"Flowers," she growls, vanishing into the kitchen.

We drink Algerian wine and talk about the furniture. The same piano piece plays again and again because no one will turn the record over. I smoke Luckies till there's nothing left to hold. Dinner (spaghetti with mussels) is easier since the woman from NPR gets going and everyone can relax and be mute. She asks if Israeli men aren't naturally legalistic and oppressive, doesn't wait for the answer. Dessert is by the oncologist, bread pudding soaked in sherry. I imagine the stout girl alone in her dorm room; she methodically finishes a box of cinnamon doughnuts, then makes herself throw up.

Barbara serves coffee and I see that glitter again which I'd taken for the effect of snow. I wonder if authenticity is something she worries about in her writing. "How about a game of Botticelli?" she says.

We pretend not to hear.

Sue Willens is terribly horny, repeats this confidence to everyone as if she's trying to borrow five dollars.

ALICE stayed in all weekend. "It wasn't so depressing. I made cupcakes and read up on Watteau."

I untie the green ribbon and peel away Saran Wrap. With rainbow sprinkles, Alice has outlined a steep profile in the icing.

"Watteau at twenty," she explains.

One by one I pick off the sprinkles, swallow them whole.

This morning, looking for someplace to park, I watched a dutiful student strap on a shiny black motorcycle helmet, and in it, for just a second before he rode away, a distorted reflection of trees. I thought: Corey wore a helmet, but it didn't protect his head. Then I repeated this aloud and my speech condensed on the window. I should get the heater fixed.

"Baking," Alice says, "baking is not an art."

I have removed all components of the head, but the shape is still distinct in their oblong tracks, a pattern: Cut on dotted line. I smear and smooth the icing with my thumb. Inside, I make what seems to be a point: You are so complacent you don't even regret it. But I can't repeat this one out loud. Alice, back turned, is watching me.

Darker than usual, heavier, the river could divide two disputed zones. Curfew patrol, interrogation by broom handle —just pictures that we know. Out of the car, I walk about, peer. Snow tires hum above on the bridge decking. The SX-70 slides easily out of last year's gift box. Before pushing down, I close my eyes. Green Dumpster. Standpipe. Rust-streaked wall. Loading bay with pallets. I watch them pass from yellow haze to unilateral form. History condensed to a minute is wrong.

More chemical tampering, and we'll pay for it all. I spread treated squares across the hood; they're so shiny against crackled blue paint, like artificial food. With black tape from the trunk, I stick each picture to its subject: nametags. Hello, I'm . . .

Too bad you can't see them from the road.

———

I DON'T have the kind of mentality (acquisitive, analytical) that I need for my job. This revelation comes, uselessly, every few days. I put on lipstick, wipe it off before sucking at coffee I know will burn me. The active life-style, the impossible dream —just slogans that we know. Corey's father called this morning for advice, and I gave some.

"He can't relive his childhood, but you can."

It's snowing again and the car won't start. Barbara will already have left and Alice lives too far away; a cab to school means twelve or fifteen dollars.

Why shouldn't they believe I've got the flu? But I have to double over on the bed, hack into the phone. Behind my complacent scrim, I could be a cheap broad in no time. A luxury? Then I'm under the covers with my boots on, scanning an Italian design magazine. Right now the stout girl is taking vitamins. Barbara, on the highway, composes paragraphs in her head. A minitractor plows the campus drive. Chrome twinkles in Milan. The river folds.

I want to swirl in a great black cape, but I only have the lining. And Fridays.

S LOW G ROUNDER

●

U P or down, in motion or asleep
and half asleep, Speed has the
same musical questions that slosh in his head. How could you
play twelve years in the majors and end up like this? Did you
go stupid on purpose? Where is the curly wife birdfeeding you
popcorn tinged with lipstick? And the little girls begging to
stand on your big feet to be danced in circles? The Barca-
lounger? The riding mower? The tropical aquarium? Going,
going, all long gone.

So now Speed has transistor radios in his place, on sills
and ledges, hanging by wrist straps from bedpost and cabinet
knob, on top of the fridge and the toilet tank. They have silver
aerials that always point up. They have leather casings that
snap over the top like overalls; or go naked in turquoise Jap
plastic. Below, their countable speaker dots and on top a grid
of numbers make super dominoes. Very advanced. Dominoes
from Outer Space.

But even playing all together so Lurtsema downstairs
spears his ceiling with a mop handle, they can't drown out

Speed's musical questions. What happened to the four-bedroom house with skylight and sundeck? To the Chrysler New Yorker with gray velour upholstery Kimmie called mouseskin, chanting it at her sister and bouncing?

Back in Dakota, when he was still Russell and a boy, there'd been Gramp in his chair. Gramp clicking his plates on the stem of a cold pipe. Gramp in full expectation, bird gun across his knees, and sooner or later the door would suck open on a winter-crazed redskin come to take, and let him reach for one potato or lump of coal, Gramp would blast him back across the frozen porch.

You were supposed to be on guard, block the plate. But Speed had his chest protector on backwards, or something. Now he's getting the razz. The hotfoot and the horselaugh. "This bum," and he can see his picture coming down in delis and barbershops. Bumhood like something he could pass over wire so the guys duck out when he calls. "Going south for the tarpon, Speed. Keep in touch." Even his roomie four years with the Sox saying, "I'm kind of extended now, Speed. Maybe you could put it in a letter," then hanging up before he can get the address. And what had him extended was a thing called Bob's Bag-O-Salad, three of them opened around Philadelphia there, the shaved lettuce and carrots, so on, in a special plastic bag you could eat out of, then throw away, and the dressing faucets, your choice of ten. People were flocking to the greens, trying to ward off cancer.

Back in Dakota one year when he was visiting for Christmas, the wind had come down off the Canadian plains to swirl snow and dirt into what they called a "snirt" storm. It clattered against the house. Mom said, "Hardly recognize you in those clothes." Pop said, warily lifting his present, "Is it something to eat?" Pop had been three years at the Colorado School of Mines. As a cook. It was still snirting the next day and the day after that. "That dog can't but hardly see," Pop said. Perry Como sang about mistletoe and Mom sniffled. Speed went to the cellar. He put his hands in the bin of seed potatoes. Things can live in the dark, he thought, and didn't feel any better.

Speed gets out his fourteen gum cards, still shiny. Twelve full seasons, plus the one in front when they sent him down to Asheville for seasoning, and the one in back when they said you're not in our plans for this year. But we could let you be a batting coach in the Bean Dip League. He remembers the Fargo girl who sent pictures of herself on a horse, or in her band uniform. "Carry me up there and hit the big one." And the one night he puts her in his pocket Fuentes throws a no-hitter. Sandi, with a heart over the *i*. He thinks about pictures as a residue of time. "Adams led the club last year in RBIs."

Back in tenth grade in Dakota, geometry had calmed him down. Nothing he knew was so pure as those angles and arcs. Not even the hiss of a fastball inside the four points of a diamond. He made figures with compass and ruler and colored them in. Numbers might be a trick, but he could understand the laws of shape.

It's almost dark outside, so Speed turns some radios on. The sound is tight, a pressure leak, but Speed hears his questions the same. And what they want is the clacking logic of one domino tipping the next one as it falls and the next and the next and the next. But all he can remember is what the things were, not why or where they went. From the couch to the john to the bed is the only geometry left. The lines don't really meet, okay.

Noticing the buzzer, he can tell its been going some time

behind his radios. Getting up, he feels light, light as paper, when the door sucks open on a man with silver eyes, skin with a rubbery shine, and where the ears ought to be, holes in a circle like the mouthpart of a telephone.

He says, "Bless my stars."

Speed says come on in, but the shape of the doorframe seems to make him nervous. He tries to smile and it's like something he had to learn in a hurry.

Nodding to the radios: "You're a listener."

Speed shrugs a little. Those eyes are really terrible.

"So you're ready to go, then?"

Speed doesn't say, "I don't care if I never come back." He sings it.

"Really very nice there." The man gestures vaguely, impatiently. "All the lines meet. It's very forgiving."

Speed really wants him to come in now, but the man says he needs to run a couple or errands first.

"My vehicle's parked on the roof. Wait here."

Okay. In the kitchen Speed empties a can of Hormel chili into a pan. Hearing the traffic report is nice. He breaks two eggs into the pot, stirs. It doesn't require a look to know there are bits of shell in there. But so why take them out?

Ruby Dawn, Private Duty Nurse

●

S K Y disappeared from Bay City at this time of year and the lighthouse never went out. Foam crackled like burnt candy at the edges of the beach. Nightfall came as a relief. She sighed. She leaned into the casement and felt her own pulse. There was muzzle steam from dogs fighting in the yard. There were newspaper bits spinning in the wind. She turned back to the room and a white beam squared across her eyes like M-G-M key lighting.

——

S H E ' D spent December on an alcoholic case, a cartoonist who lived at the Forest Park Inn, a relentless man. He seemed able to breathe up gin from out of the air. On Christmas Day they ate chicken pot pies. He made her portrait on a napkin, told jokes, sang Gershwin. He said, "This is the A material, buttercup." He raged, wept, and went to sleep at last.

She called the rich uncle, said, "I'm only a nurse. I can't stop him from killing himself."

Now she was on a palsy case, a lady author who lived on the top floor of the Tarleton Arms with Turkish carpets and a Siamese cat. Attempting a new book, the old lady could dictate only one chapter.

One day it would begin: *This was the morning it was meant to happen, and I lay there trembling with nervous antici- pation, with excitement I should have been saving for the climax, lay there as darkness faded slowly from the window and the sounds of a sullen city came up . . .*

And the next time: *Rusty woke up knowing he was going to kill her, as surely as the morning insects hummed in their grassy retreats, as birds sang each to each, palm fronds trembled in a nervous breeze . . .*

And then: *The first shaft of sunlight to pierce the mul- lioned windows found Dr. McCoy still at work, poised with excitement over the cluttered oaken table . . .*

And it would go on and on without ever reaching a period.

She still felt pride, walking out in her navy-blue cape, red enamel Medic Cadet pin shining over the clasped collar. Her steps echoed off the row-house fronts. Mist curled over slag piled by the tracks. Then came the warmth of her own address, ribbed brown rubber matting on the stairs, that smell of radiator paint. And the single privacy of her room. She took off the hard starched cap, white lacquered shoes. She fixed a hot bath with lilac salts and alum. Her training explained that you could never really be clean, free of invisible organisms. She did not mind this. The white iron bed was drawn under the steep roof slant, by the low dormer window. Her open pores felt the weave of candy-stripe sheets. Her sleep was sweet as a fever.

———

A L L kinds of heat records were set that July. There were, every afternoon, ice-cream-and-lemonade parties for the house staff at Goriot Memorial. From balcony windows at one end of the activity room she looked out over the lawn, wilting now in the interval between morning and evening sprinkler time, at pansies and geraniums burned in their beds. She dabbed pink cupcake icing from the corners of her mouth.

"If you like this view, I know a better one."

The new surgeon had come up behind her. He was tall and broad-shouldered, with clear, inviting eyes and an insistent jaw. She clutched the railing, sick at the odor of his brilliantine.

"When I can steal a moment in the evening, I go to the rotunda, up in the dome. That was the operating theater a hundred years ago, and it saw some great medical advances. I stand there in silence, watching the moonlight, and I feel I'm in touch with a beautiful essence." He smiled. "You might like to join me some evening."

She gestured illegibly, groaned, pushed past him.

The new surgeon sucked at his cold pipe. "Well, I'll be a monkey's uncle," he said.

She went into the empty chapel and knelt to pray. Saint Dymphna looked on from a deep sconce. The martyrdom of Saint Ignatius glowed red and blue in the cusped arch window. She asked mercy for those lingering victims of the bus depot fire. She asked for clarity in her heart.

She went down in the elevator, past X-ray rooms, the pathology lab, under a geometry of asbestos-covered pipe, through the cool connecting tunnel, up gray linoleum steps to her room in the back of the dorm. Next to a buzzing fan, Mona was soaking her feet in a basin of ice water. Mona worked night shift; she was still in her pajamas.

"Hi, sleepyhead. Doing all right?"

"I'm trying to think like an Eskimo."

Mona was tiny and dark, with brown eyes under black bangs. Her people farmed a hundred fifty acres of barley and russet potatoes in Bluefield, Minnesota.

"You could fry an egg on the sidewalk out there."

"And I'm in ER. It's going to be stab wounds and psychos all night long."

She looked down into rippling water. "Why don't you let me freshen your polish?"

Mona said, "That would be fine."

She knelt and separated Mona's toes, wedging them open with cotton balls. She went at it slowly, precisely, sweat burning in her eyes. The polish, called Summer Cerise, beaded thickly at the end of the brush.

——

MRS. RADCLIFFE was dictating again, a shopping list this time.

"Tenderloin only. I want a well-marbled cut."

These incoherent moods: The old woman had snuffled and cooed while having her hair put in braids, and now she was cold and peremptory. Caprice. It could be the name of a houseboat.

"And make it white turnips, not yellow."

The old woman's tics went in their wonted series. Her hands trembled over satin robe lapels.

"They keep specially in stock for me a certain tea blend. Griffin's Limeflower."

She came out of the bright dizzy bedroom and into the hall, where it was dusk. The runner was spongy underfoot, its figures sinking away in brown wear. She went still in the front room before the wall of shelved books, their spines a vague medley. Only the ticking of the mantel clock was distinct. She turned on the lights and wrote in the chart:

"6PM—Medications administered; patient resting comfortably."

———

DISMISSED from the hospital, she went on to Ransome Hall, a brick keep under iron-ore mountains at the far side of town. Wealthy neurasthenics went to Harbor Springs or to Bois Blanc Island, while the rest came here: firebugs, cataleptics, pederasts. She worked long hours on the lockdown ward, and wasn't afraid to be by herself. Behind barred windows, she was free from niceties and rules ("No jewelry is to be worn while on duty"). There was only the rule of law, of the hammerlock and the leather restraint. She was glad to show strength instead of endurance. And when strength ran out, there was time to dream.

It was easy—they trusted her with all the keys. Light was low in the storeroom. She snapped the glass neck of the ampoule, drew its full contents up into the syringe, lifted her skirt, punctured a thigh. Brighter light fell on drifts of white flannel blanket. Poultice pans had sheen. Rubber ice caps and rubber sheets seemed slowly to breathe. Her skin was cream with a waft of vanilla.

O N her day off she went to the movies. There was a very sad story about adoption, a silly musical to fill out the bill, and a newsreel in between. While women around her cried at the feature, she sucked on root beer barrels and thought how the faces up there were no more false or true than those she remembered with wens, warts, goiters, or masked behind gauze. And then, during Movietone footage of the Miss Citrus contest, she was the only one laughing. Afterwards, she went to a tearoom for barley soup and sweet rolls. From the drugstore by the trolley stop, she bought magazines to take home. A back-cover layout announced that the latest achievement in typewriters made for writing perfection with silence. "Allows clear thinking, reduces fatigue, improves accuracy." She thought of pretty pool typists chatting together, window-shopping, and wondered if there really was any such thing as a "normal" job. Had she been missing out? Her eyes were reflected in the trolley car window, just above the condensation of her breath. She opened to a full-length novelette by someone named Anne P. Radcliffe.

"She's a lovely corpse," said the intern. Looking at the crushed girl, he knew she wasn't just another hit-and-run. He was wheeling this ambulance on the trail of murder!

A F T E R the asylum was sold for a tax judgment, she went on to Highcroft Academy, a boarding school for girls wanting individual remediation. With field hockey, tennis, riding, came sprains and contusions for treatment; there were viruses and allergies, the menorrheal, the homesick, the hysterical. The campus was large, thickly wooded, and walking out with her sweet-grass basket to gather mushrooms, she sometimes found girls necking or smoking and once, a tramp asleep in fallen leaves. Her reticence in these matters led to respect and the receipt of confidences—the ostracized girl, daughter of missionaries; the girl who stole food; the girl seduced by her grandfather; and finally the would-be suicide, her lips blue with bichloride of mercury, who sobbed, "You're the only one who cares about me, and I don't even know your first name." She could recognize that love came like gas from a hard rubber mouthpiece.

———

RID of pride, she went to the agency with a new haircut, her face rubbed plain, her hands dry and smelling of white soap.

"I want a terminal case," she said.

Miss Barton rearranged papers on her desk, frowning. "We're not here for your accommodation."

"I would wait until something was available."

She had walked all the way here, crunching rock salt on the downtown pavements. She had purpose that was no dream, though she saw it over and over in her mind.

Miss Barton pressed her thumb into a gum eraser. "Do you mind living in?"

"Not at all."

"Ever worked with a pediatric iron lung before?"

"Once or twice."

In her sleep she had peeled the last rules away, and woke

up clean. She had foreign aromas like summer cabin wood, gardenia jelly, and words brittle in her mouth as a thermometer.

"Don't be too sure of yourself," Miss Barton said.

———

SHE stares through mullioned windows at the running lights of a barge. Dogs flee from a bucket of water. Spinning newspapers come to rest, and sigh. It isn't early; it isn't late. She hears the small shy coughing and turns back into the room.

CYCLING POSTURE

●

RILEY eats out all the time because it is less sad. She moved
out on him in December; plane trees now are tipped with early
April green, but sweeping, matching socks, heating stew—
these things are still sad for him. Normally, he has dinner at
La Campaña d'Oro. They serve a beer called El Señor Presi-
dente. Sad maybe, lonesome, but he doesn't flaunt it with a
book propped against the napkin holder. He reads the menu
(Chinese on one side and Cuban on the other), always gives
the same order: *ropa vieja*, black beans, yellow rice.

And at this she would show her fine exasperation. "Don't
you have any curiosity?" And Riley would say that yes, he
did; that it was about the two Campaña families running from
Mao in '51, from Castro in '62. And he supposes now that
routines were what pushed her away.

———

R I L E Y bicycles to work because it makes him feel quick and bold and slightly European. Six miles down, six miles back. His calves are spectacular. Normally, he keeps the bike right next to his desk. Moretti doesn't complain any more.

Gravity Media publishes three monthlies (*Our True Lives, Terror/Counterterror, Global Detective*), a bimonthly (*Cat Fighters: The Journal of Female Combat*), and whenever possible, one-shots like *Amazing Pet Stories Annual*, or *Cudgo Bros. Tour Scrapbook*. Moretti, as executive president, must hustle. He has a full-time staff of only five and a distributor who can't seem to penetrate the national convenience stores. He says acts of contrition all day and drinks milk in defense of his stomach.

Riley writes everything, even captions. He writes great quantities quickly and easily; his sound is never wrong. Everyone in the office marvels. But really it is nothing special, a trick rather than a gift, a type of accidental serenity. His lacks make it possible: a lack of ambition, a lack of taste, and—he must admit—a lack of curiosity; that is to say, of a curiosity immediately engaged. He operates always at several removes, straggling, aimed elsewhere. This is fine. All under the city there is furious burrowing: cabbies just short of a doctorate, waitresses studying with Merce Cunningham. Riley is grateful to be spared.

Today, for *OTL*, before even removing his parka, he does "I Joined an Abortion Club" and "My Daughter Is Trying to Kill Me."

———

ACCORDING to his only source, her niece, a sous-chef, she's gone to look after her Connecticut grandfather. Will her name and the town's be enough on the envelope? He fills three pages, but it's a letter to someone else. He looks at the perforations of a stamp and wonders how they are made.

Watching *Million Dollar Movie* is sad also. How she would fill in dialogue of her own, hang on the most obvious plots. Her lips pulled back in concentration, like safety padding over crooked teeth. He gets up to look for the nail clipper, orders himself back down. To make this into the pathos that comes quickly and easily, he tries to think what her grandfather is thinking.

The bedroom is an oblong perpendicular to the hall. A single window, off center, overlooks the street. From this height it is barely possible to read an address painted on a trash can. A mirror is the oldest thing in the room, its silvering eaten away at two corners. Under the bed, in a chronology of blue, yellow, white, are hardened knobs of Kleenex. The clock face glows in the dark.

———

RILEY studies while riding. The texts of cycling posture: racers sleek and low over their handlebars veer in and out of the traffic pack; casuals pedal with arms folded, rock to bunge-corded radios; dutifuls stiff-armed and high in the saddle badge themselves with filtration masks, crash helmets. Riley, though, is a neutral, his three-speed unfashionably thick, his text pared to one word: conveyance. Passing over the invariable route—down Ninth Avenue, east on Fourteenth Street, the bins of cook pots and rubber sandals already pawed through, south again on Broadway—he holds in mental foreground his image of the wheeling masses of Beijing.

Moretti snaps pencils; he pleads and paces. T/C has to be at the typesetter's by three, and Riley has just now begun the feature. "PLO Using Mind Control." Riley abandons his lead, rolls in a fresh sheet. Moretti groans. Mrs. Vega, the Subscription Department, goes downstairs for more milk.

Lina comes out of the file room, biting her lip.

Riley glances. "How recently were they used?"

"Three issues ago. But I can crop differently."

With the Pratt students who come in to do paste-up, Lina is the Art Department.

"This one—the hands out—I thought might go as a psychic trance."

Lina is so dark: her eyes, hair, skin, a round depth to her voice. She is very small, very serious. She wears plain black clothes. Her people are Calabrese.

"I don't know. He looks ill."

Lina and Riley would sleep together, but thinking about it, they agree, is better. The work abets. Editing, doing captions at opposite ends of a desk, they are thinking about it all the time.

"No panic. I'll look some more."

And Lina adores her husband, who is shy because of his faulty English, blind in one eye and retired from boxing.

Riley finishes just before two and goes for lunch. Wendell, the Advertising Department, takes him for pastrami, then talks too much to eat. The great Park Row press wars. The scoops, hoaxes, flash bars.

"See? It was right out there."

Wendell points to the corner cut-rate luggage store.

Probably it had once been a saloon; possibly an editor had been shot in the doorway over a love nest scandal. But Wendell lives with his mother and romances a time before he was born. He is as hopeful as anyone wanting to add bustline inches, to lose weight while sleeping. Transformation is real to him. Instant $$$—song poems wanted. Sharpen saws at home—be your own boss.

Riley says, "I bet there isn't a thing you'd rather be doing."

Wendell grins, tips heavily.

Too many coffees at La Campaña. The caffeine, the glucose . . . Riley's problem is not his inability to sleep but the lack of a routine to meet the situation. He tries crossword puzzles, a hot bath. The muscle strips along his spine are cramping and he cannot distract himself. "Scared" is the wrong word, but he wishes the phone would ring.

———

H E signs in, and the guard, without shifting his eyes from *Muhammad Speaks*, runs him up in the cage. There are brass fixtures in the Starrett Building someone still takes time to polish. Riley believes in the marble, that it isn't something else finished to look like marble. He goes up two flights, down the long shadow of a hall, turning, as if on a dance floor, to face each frosted pane, bowing. Mail Exchange. School of Fashion. Loan Broker. Patent Attorney. To punch out the glass to see what's inside. So Riley feels his curiosity engaged and does not like it.

He keys both locks of the Gravity office, waters the plant, feeds Mrs. Vega's angelfish, makes soup from a packet. It is still dark outside, untinged. He goes to the farthest room back, sits under bright lights, against bundles of *Air Disaster!*, a "Collector's Item" on coated paper, and blows ripples in the soup.

Breathless and overgroomed, Moretti arrives at eight-thirty, takes a few minutes to be surprised.

"You're not supposed to be in. And where's that bike?"

His face is at once pallid and aggressive; he might be wearing Kabuki makeup. "You're the cog, Riley, so we keep turning. Stand still in this business, you know . . ."

Moretti has been in sportswear, outdoor advertising, an adult motel. Now finally, with the magazines, he is making a go. Perhaps this does not agree with him.

Lina is so tiny she has to buy schoolgirl sizes, like this sappy pleated skirt. But she is so grave in it. Lina sits on the edge of her desk, where Riley has been typing since dawn.

"Early," she says.

Riley looks down. Her feet barely reach the handle of the middle drawer. She is wearing Mary Janes.

"I needed some extra time for thinking."

Lina smiles, touches his first page of copy, "Nebraska's Pantyhose Strangler," smiles, nods.

———

A LITTLE after ten, Riley collapses onto the sofa Wendell brought up from the street and crammed into his office. Hopeful Wendell. He is on the phone trying to land a major for *OTL*. They are coming out with a line of feminine towelettes. And neuroelectric fatigue twitches for Riley, fragments of "Gay

Bikers' Homicide Cookout" that he hasn't written yet, and stickpin revival (Wendell's bulging Park Row vests) without the scars from molten lead for type, and seeing Angelina, old and dried under her full name, blinking through Catanzaro street dust, sucking Fanta orange from a cup. This is Riley's quality of mind when working, elaborative; and true, he controls in part, moving here to there like a photo stylist. But distance is lost, his removes collapsed and overrun. Awful, this layered weight on him, like something made up and come round, revenge of his written victims giving back what he'd stuck them with. He turns away from clatter, Wendell's tricked face, into the cushions. "Scared" is now the word, even as he falls asleep.

Riley arrives at his decision prismatically, that is to say by a kind of bending. Bicycling to Connecticut to see her is not a sound idea. But once he has formed it, he must complete it, in order to avoid in the future looking back on the torpor and cowardice of a failure to carry through. Regret—no, thank you. Regret is why people read what he writes.

Things to take: map, tools, food and drink, fresh shirt. But Riley just carries his bike downstairs and begins. Excellent. This is the spontaneous thing to do. Pedaling steadily through the night, he should arrive Saturday morning, not so early and not so late. Perfect.

She will have to let him stay, out of respect for the gesture. He will be cool and mysterious, only hint at his pain. Perhaps she will have a few admissions to make. There will be daffodils. Kneeling to cut some, she will turn her head, smile crookedly into the sun, and his hand under her chin, lifting . . . It will be like nothing he could write.

Turning onto Route 33 at Wilton, Riley is very tired. His

memory reaches doubt: A dozen pages short on *CF*, out of time. And when Riley asked, okay. She and her niece stripped to their underwear, took to the floor in genre grapple poses, hair-pulling, all of it. He shot three rolls of black-and-white (ASA 200) with a borrowed Minolta. And Moretti said, "Man, great stuff. I mean these girls really hate each other."

What had Riley missed?

He walks the bike now, counting down the even numbers of Beadle Street. Green gutters and trim, the man at the Texaco said. Not a very big town, his mental picture ludicrous against it. No stately spaces here. Everything is shoved down. The daffodils are plastic.

"Why?" she says, and again, quietly, "why?"

But she steps back from the door to let him in.

"I biked all the way."

Why had he thought it would sound impressive?

"It's all right," she says, seeing how he peers. "They came from the Center to take him for a ride."

Won't she go change out of her pajamas, or put coffee on? Riley can't look at her, instead substitutes the painting of JFK and John XXIII against fleecy clouds, Jordan almonds in a shell dish. He smooths his hands together.

"Honest to God, Riley, you seem right at home. So what're you doing here?"

He looks at her, breathing carefully. Did she sleep in all that makeup or just put it on?

They sit on the porch drinking Cokes. Her long legs are stretched out across the railing. The air is still.

"Your problem is you look at home anyplace because nothing stands out." She says this solicitously, as though he might see a doctor about it. "It's like the day I knew we were

going to split was when Nina and me did those wrestling pictures. You remember? I go, 'Well, he might want to do something after, with both of us.' Not like I wanted you to, though
probably it would've been okay. But naturally, you wouldn't
even think of it. No curiosity."

"It was an assignment for work."

Her eyes are closed; she's not listening. Riley could shake
up the Coke with his thumb over the hole and . . .

A man across the street is getting set to clip his hedge.
First he goes inside with the long orange cord so he can plug
in. Two little girls scream in the spray of a hose, taking turns.
Somebody ordered a cab; the driver honks, honks, but no one
comes.

She says: "Go down and get some rye bread, I'll make
sandwiches." Her eyes are still closed.

Riley's legs are so tired that it's a joy to pedal. The store
is cool and empty. He gets a Slurpee, and bubble gum packaged
like chewing tobacco. Magazines are every which way in the
rack. *Hit Paraders* and *Playgirls* and *Omnis* and *Motor Trends*
and *Cavaliers* and one sun-faded *Global Detective* from last
June. "Artist Model Drowns in Punchbowl," one of his favor-
ites. He goes out into the sun and sits on the curb to read.

PHOSPHATES

●

CONLAN bounced in the Ford and his fresh cigarette rolled under the pedals. He tried to stamp out the coal and lurched. How could the road be so muddy and still bounce him? Conlan was no scientist, that he'd grant. Breath plumed out of his mouth, made a milky blue patch on the windshield. His tongue was dry. It wanted to taste raspberry.

"Mutual trust," Mr. Tunbridge said every September. "That's what makes the stars come out."

And then he gave Conlan something in advance.

——

"MULLED cider, cocoa, herb teas," the brother said in answer to the question of how he could keep his soda fountain open through the winter.

Conlan looked up and down the street, which had only two summers ago been paved. "Herb teas," he repeated. "You're dreaming."

"People need a wholesome place to come," the brother said. "After the sleigh ride, after the skaters' party. And the community sing. That's every week."

"You're a bloody public servant now?" Conlan spat with finesse. "You'll put bloody marshmallows in the cocoa, and no extra charge."

The brother was waiting for the Syracuse truck that brought him gassed water.

"And what would you have me do, then? Go out on the lake with you and fish through the ice?"

"Nah, you'd find a way to drown."

Conlan felt his nose going red in the sun. The street was giving up vapors.

——

EVERYTHING was bare, except for the oaks, always the last to let go. The birches were right without leaves, their black limbs striping the white sky, their white paper bark mottled black. Conlan viewed uncreased gray water through them, the lake, Racquet Lake, which the Tunbridges could have named after themselves, but hadn't, which they owned in some different way than their ore mountains and smelters and ships. More intimately, more seriously. Conlan went into the boathouse. He looked at the racked canoes, smelled varnish. His palms felt cold; his fingers tingled and twitched as if he had just held someone under, fatally.

——

FOR a living, the brother had cut wood and shot quail and hung windows and so on. People in the town liked his thrift.

Then he wooed and won Miss Loretta Frame, who had served eight years as governess to the younger Tunbridge children, and they liked his sand. The brother had foresight, and was not ashamed. His fountain had a veined marble counter, checkered floor tiles, filigreed taps and faucets, an etched blue mirror, and in their season, fresh flowers at every table. Father Voss, the Lutheran, who liked a tulip sundae, said the brother's place was so comfortable it made him think about retirement. The brother had to have new dentures, he smiled so much. Conlan wasn't exactly jealous; but he was irritated. It was weak to take the money. He told Loretta the children wept whenever her name was mentioned.

———

T H E Tunbridge family carried history the way soda carried the colors of syrup. They knew things by instinct.

Riker, the in-law whose cups of tea were always laced, lectured on eugenics at Cornell. While the rest of the family was under sail, racing one another from cove to cove, Riker stayed uncoaxable in shade, painting the wicker.

"I read in this morning's paper," he said, "of Mrs. Elise Winch of Oneida being bitten by an owl. She was only thirty-four."

Inside the house, in the hexagonal library on the third floor, where planets were painted in color on the ceiling, the skull of Garrison Tunbridge, Sr., who found copper in Wyoming and guano in Peru, was displayed under glass.

"One must expand or go mad," said Auntie Vera, who could dance in Italian.

Conlan imagined the nests of hair under her arms.

———

THUNDER rolled away across the northern scarp. Hat brims dripped and shingles glistened. Inside the rain-battered cups of columbine and tiger lily, bees died of exhaustion.

"Lemon phosphate."

"Cherry phosphate."

The twins exchanged looks in the blue mirror. Their faces were as identical as their coifs, bicycles, leg-of-mutton sleeves.

"With ice, please," they said.

The temperature swing brought on by the storm made the brother ill. His skin was clammy and he trembled. With disagreeable vividness came recollection of the home left near forty years ago, tea and treacle by a peat fire.

"And extra straws."

The matched white faces looming, dead white under freckles.

———

AS Conlan swept the porch, he heard stones click in the lapping water. The lake at its deepest was said to be twelve hundred feet. It was terribly cold there and all the fish were blind. The music room and parlor, as Conlan peered through the windows, seemed deep in that forbidding way. He shivered, imagining the piano keys' slick cold like some ancient ice unpleasantly preserved. Red-brown geometrics floated up. He turned away, mouth curling around the taste of foreign carpet.

———

L O R E T T A said, "This is the weekend I go to New York."

The brother understood about interest on a loan.

"I'll need new pajamas," he said.

He took his wife to the station with an hour to spare. Alone on the platform, they watched and were watched by a murder of crows.

"Your brother," Loretta began.

Desperately inspired, her husband emptied his pockets of change, fell on his knees to retrieve it, and she pointed out coins with the triangular toe of her boot.

"Phone me tonight," he said.

She smiled from the compartment window, pretending not to hear, subtle as tailings.

———

" H E L P yourself, Conlan," said G.T., Jr.

The squash were enormous, the cucumbers ready to explode. Tunbridge, in pressed green overalls and striped engineer's hat, enhanced a proprietary gleam. He was proud of the family fertilizer, a secret blend. Knowing the invitation as otherwise meant—he was free to take, but invisibly, please— Conlan still bit a tomato, inhaling seed clumps like frog eggs, only warm. Tunbridge caught the gesture, but maintained his gleam, sharpened it.

"We used to call them love apples," he said. "A member of the nightshade family."

———

O B S E S S I V E L Y, the brother thought about sherbet. He stared out the bay window, past his backwards name in gold paint shaded with black. The street stayed empty, the main street without a policeman to patrol it. Azalea sherbet? Rosemary? Mushroom? French monks had recipes, and sultans did. Knowledge was money, history was money, and so on. The brother wiped the marble counter until he could see himself wiping. The veins in the marble, unlike the veins in the body, were confused and led nowhere. Blue veins in orderly fashion shipped blood the color of sherbet, an essence. If fact was fact and the street was empty, why not a supernatural sherbet? One that removed the power of speech and made music.

———

I T felt safest to enter by the kitchen. The Ford refused to turn over in the falling chill, and now Conlan was inside the house, drawn to white surfaces—cupboards, stove, and sink— which made the most of last light. But he heard things like dance steps on the lake and voices from under the carpet. Conlan had always understood the way of being alone, and to lose that would leave him with nothing. When he stole something from the house last summer, it had been a little picture book that no one would miss; it had been a gesture for himself alone. Pictures had nothing behind them, were only themselves. We would miss you, Conlan. He began searching every drawer for candles.

MUNICIPAL NOIR

●

MADRID, in Nebraska's south-west corner, in the wide ter-raced plain below the Platte, had a Hog & Hominy Fest annually until 1978. There are three taverns in the town, two hardware stores, a Boys' Club, a pistol range, and Strunk Fabrication, where crèche figures and baptismal fonts are made by a system of injection molding.

———

IN August of 1977, Ron Maddox was planning a future there. He had come to his wife's country from North Dakota. Ron's Pythagoras ABM Silo Group Commander, Lieutenant Benkel-man, had been the best man at the wedding in Minot. Bonnie was expecting a child, but she wasn't pregnant yet.

———

IT was only the fact of having once received a Visible Man anatomy doll for Christmas that prepared Kallinger for what he was to find all over the kitchen of Unit No. 6 at the mobile home park just off the county blacktop midway between Madrid and La Paz. Interim Coroner Perk Feed had so little to work with that even a preliminary finding seemed unlikely. Feed's right leg was some two and one quarter inches shorter than his left, due to a fraternity initiation.

———

W A S Fran the kind of woman who would go all the way to Yankton for bridgework? Why had Lute Strunk rotated his best acres into sorghum? His CB handle was "Fledermaus," and some said he had peculiar ideas about Jews.

———

A T 9:15 a.m. on Friday, Miss Clara Musil reported that her collection of little glass animals had been vandalized by a one-armed man. The light-blue hatchback had been abandoned next to the Elks Hall. Both Reverend and Mrs. LaFollette were treated for hyperventilation.

———

K A L L I N G E R , at the subsequent awards dinner, wearing a strap-in-the-back "Go 'Huskers" baseball cap, refused to eat his portion of tapioca pudding until someone had tasted it first, and later proposed a curious toast "to Negro banking interests."

———

" HE wanted the best of both worlds," said a bureau insider.

Donna, Benkelman's estranged wife, disagrees. Living in San Diego now, she has legally adopted Fran's two sons and works as a commercial illustrator.

"Gas spectrometry is fine. Fiber analysis is fine. But people want a good, human story, and in this case they didn't get it."

———

SUSPICION of multiple sodomy focused on a "drifter" with a history of bronchiectasis. Someone had caused Jud Musil's feed troughs to be infected with hog cholera. These were theories congruent with mutual distrust.

"We lacked a fallback position," one resident later observed. "Pictures just didn't tell the story."

———

AND then on a crisp October morning, during the final hour of Ingo Feed's *Stop & Swap* radio show, a strangely insistent man phoned in to offer his entire collection of bat-wing fans in exchange for "the global freezing design."

———

BY now people were beginning to ask hard questions about the investigative reporter in their midst. Complicitous terrorist supplying atrocity photos to clients in Melbourne, Rome, Pernambuco, and Dubai? Semiliterate impostor becalmed in a delusional world of *Mod Squad* reruns?

———

OVER treacherous, ice-glazed roads, normally temperate, circumspect farm families drove the forty-five miles to Arbeiter Mall so they could dine at a Polynesian restaurant. Owner Gus Triandos would boast once too often about his acquaintance with high-level research. The baby back ribs were moist, tender, imaginatively sauced.

———

TRIAL proceedings, convened at the county seat of Bogota, began the first week of the new year under the guidance of Judge Pangloss LaFollette, no relation.

Dr. Shah, for the prosecution, explained that, as an "outsider," he'd had little success in convincing the authorities, even in the face of corroborative evidence from a degreed caseworker, that the dozens of cigarette burns on the chest were cause for alarm. Dr. Zweig, for the defense, described Ron as "a man without qualities." Fran, according to the testimony of a Chicago psychic, was operating a barge on the Loire.

———

"QUITE simply, there are no words to describe what Mrs. Maddox has already paid in suffering," said a friend of the family.

———

BONNIE appeared each day in the same oyster-gray ensemble, occupied the same front-row seat. Her only change of expression, a slight moue disarranging normally serene features, came as a result of Kallinger's breakdown on the stand, his admission that "I never learned to hit the curveball."

———

THE jury, perhaps overly sequestered, imposed its inability to reach a verdict.

F RYED C UTLETS

by
Rico V. Poons

[Biographical Note: Rico V. Poons (born Abe Attel) was a member of the New York State Legislature, for Ulster County, from 1948 until 1955. In November of that latter year, he told companions at a Slide Mountain hunting camp to "deal me out while I go write in the snow." He was never seen again.

Poons' only other published work, "The Otter That Swam in the Soup," appeared, in two parts, in the fortnightly *Lads' Gazette* for June 23rd and July 8th, 1917, at which time the author was eleven years old.]

●

H ERE is the Club Onyx, at the same location thru two World Wars. The house band has a contract with Decca. The complementary matchbooks were designed by a cousin of Reginald Marsh.

——

H E R E is Snuffy Howe, of the Bar Harbor Howes, the all-Ivy wressler with pins in both knees, a Stage Door Johnny with a heavy portfolio.

——

W H I L E studying at Brown, Snuffy took employment with the Mastic Gum Co. of Providence. For them he composed a series of Trading Cards titled "Cameos Of American Conversation." He still carries a specimen in his wallet, #18 in a series of 50.

> The Blizzard Of '88 . . . Only two men had ventured thru the driving snow and wind to partake of their customerry noon repast at The Murray Hill Chop House. These stanch men, Scanlon, a hotelier, and Shapiro, a tunesmith, sat in complete silence until the fowl was served, Capon With Currant Sauce.
>
> Shapiro: Nothing goes straight to the heart like good food.
> Scanlon: I never met a man to say no.
> Shapiro: Not for all the rice in China.

——

H E R E is Dodie at the hatcheck stand, singing to herself about honeysuckle vines and tall sugar pines. She walks to work 37 blocks from her flat on Terpsichore Street. There her drapes

are festive with donkeys and watermelons embroydered on. She
has a closetful of shoes. Dodie collects footwear of all kinds.
And who *doesn't* tell she looks like Betty Hutton—everybody's
Jitterbugging Daughter, ooo yess, and the girl who made the
Miracle At Morgan's Creek.

———

H E R E is the band at a long table in the Onyx kitchen. They
are eating elk wieners and kraut, drinking ale. Guido (C-
Melody Sax) says he is the only person to ever go broke on
Florida Real Estate. A kid making roux for the Gumbo burns
himself bad.

———

O N L Y one customer at the bar, Chick Lazslo, the City Hall
Reporter. He's been snooping for scandle all day, and no luck.
He's drinking rock-and-rye doubles, and pretending to be in
Afrika. Over the backbar there's a desert landscape, lozenge
shapes and minarets under a red sun, basic-ly. Like the artist
got swacked on a carton of Camels.

———

H E R E ' S this gnarly Cop poking his nitestick into the big
man sleeping on a bench at the RR station. The big man rubs
his black face and sits up. His clawhammer coat is torn and
his shoes are somewhere else. He rubs his great low-thumbed
meathooks together and smiles. This is Snuffy Howe, the Bar

Harbor scion and range pistol champ. Snuffy Howe is a Gorilla.

——

J A N U A R Y , '26, and the Turley Howes are returned from their Afrikan rubber plantation to the castle overlooking the textile mills on the river. It has been snowing furtive-ly for days, and it looks like Connecticut or Michigan or Pennsylvania from the window of a bus. Dr. Livesy, a GP of the very first water, sexologist, fly fisherman, and Ambassador-To-Be, wears his pince-nez on a ribbon. He calls for boiling vinegar and arranges instruments on a tray, chaynsmoking as he works. After the long delivery, they read the papers and don't say a thing. Mrs. Howe stops crying and hangs herself.

——

H E R E is the hexagonal brass check Snuffy receives in exchange for his Borsalino. Dodie looks into his sunken black eyes. He tells her they could be First in History to be married underwater. How's about Chesapeake Bay? Dodie says, well, anyway, you look durable enough. And the way she says it is so offhand, like she's home frying up some cutlets and a little cigarette ash falls in the pan.

——

B E T W E E N sets Doghouse Riley (Bass Fiddle) creeps into the pantry to glom some reefer. The only thing he can smell is sacked onions. Doghouse is thinking with his voice he ought to throw over this nowhere gig and move into radio. He experiments with some intros: From the Fabulous Assagai Room . . . Vulcan Tire Radio Breaks in With the News!

―――

R I G H T behind him, between the onions and the wall, Dodie's satin heels are hooked over the furred Howe shoulders on which the future of a Dynasty rests. She says in his ear: I've never had anybody like you. And no Sweet Talk here, but a matter of fact. Like she's telling her butcher to trim off the fat.

―――

H E R E is the enormous Solaryum of Marmalade Hospital, an aroma of moss, a canopy of fronds. Dr. Livesy, still sharp in his 90's (he is allowed to treat himself), arrives for an interview with Mr. Lazslo of The Bugle. Absolutely, son, always a head for figures. Could have been Mr. Memory in the Vaudeville. Reciting imagined names and addresses, false bank account numbers, he rolls the gift cigar between acid-scarred fingers.

―――

O N NBC's "Metropolitan Matinee," a new Decca release is having its Debut. Dodie sings the little eight-bar piano break, and all the reed parts. Crouching on the bathroom tile, she oyls her new riding boots from Snuffy, and the feel of it makes her heart pound.

―――

PLANE trees are dropping their leaves in the park. The nannys in the playground are erect and unsmiling. Snuffy Howe, the Milk Fund Man of the Year, climbs down from his sleeping nest and cannot remember where he is. He inspects fresh manure on the bridle path, drinks water from a stump, using wadded grass as a sponge. Crouching, alert, he watches men hoping for the price of breakfast pitch pennys at a wall.

HIGHSPEED
LINEAR MAIN ST.

●

THE darkroom is a good place to work on my theory that electrons move faster as you travel south towards the Equator. Four rolls of Tri-X are turning slowly in developer, part of the project out of which my tangent theory came like a bee from the hive. Am I going too fast?

I meant to track on film and in words, improvisationally, the New York–Key West highway experience. Note the verb tense. Germ idea and what it becomes through process should be discrete.

Already you will be wanting context. Fair enough. I am a man in early middle age, precise to a fault in my habits, but given no less to loose talk. My marriage is nine years old. I am lugubrious; Daphne is the one with the fizz. She likes me to threaten her over the phone. I am happy to do this.

The serial windshield narrative makes lists.

Wigwam Village	molded fiberglass colossi	Caves of Mystery
auto bazaar	Big Boy	Tile Town
dinosaur park	Tower of Pizza	chalet motel
Toto's	Zeppelin Diner	drive-thru bank

I know that tempo is important and I constantly watch the clock. Looking a magazine over, I calculate how many minutes it will take to read this or that article. Normally, I will have the TV on as well and possibly be talking on the phone. Daphne says, unfairly, that I'm afraid to sit still and concentrate. But I am well known for hand-tinted still-life arrangements.

Modus operandi: montage, collage, bricolage.

scratch 'n' sniff stickers
fruit-shaped gumballs
rubber animals
copper jewelry
pocket guides
budget tapes
cedar boxes
pennants
ashtrays
keyrings
posters
decals

Art is a business, but not so the reverse. I talk on the phone, have lunch, that's it. I don't sleep with curators.

On the phone to Daphne, I speak in a natural voice.

"Believe it. Frankie knows how to put edge on a knife. Thin oil and a smooth stone."

I often call from the booth in the Ramayana while my koftas, dal, and chapatis are being prepared. This booth is right next to the kitchen; its aromas inspire me. Later, when I'm having coffee, Preva or Subash, one of the brothers, will sit down with me to talk. They share my Salem Lights and ask me to clarify words. Recently, the brothers have invested in a record label. "Picture wallah," one of them will say. "We are confused by 'rock the house.'" I try to caution them, but they will not be cautioned. The label, dealing in rap music only, has offices in Jersey City.

Painting has destroyed "landscape," and left us with "map."

Trenton	onion rings
Havre de Grace	crabcakes
Virginia Beach	sausage po' boy
Greenville	chess pie
Savannah	drop biscuits
Opa-Locka	moros y cristianos

I like to draw parallels. Daphne calls this "laying track." I reply that converging rails teach perspective to small children. Perhaps, Daphne says, this is why as adults their definitions blur. Stella, our daughter, is six and takes no side.

"I'm *sooo* exhausted," she says, collapsing theatrically at our feet.

But of course, right there, by posing she makes a parallel, an alter ego.

Daphne says, "Mimicry is not analogy."

Yes, we are being insufferable. Lunch resumes with humorless laughter; the salad dressing features basil from our window box, the coffee is brewed very dark.

"Stella! Will you come out from under the table?"

"Just as a for instance," I begin. My wife chews grimly. Are these the glinting eyes I fell in love with? "Just as a for instance, isn't it amazing that at one time in Ireland they bled their cows to mix with milk just as the Masai do in Kenya today?"

"No."

When Daphne has the last word, it is usually of one syllable.

park-way n. a broad roadway bordered by trees and shrubs. (soften curves, plantings to guard from dazzle and wind, harmonize design)
free-way n. a multi-lane divided highway with fully controlled access.
(eliminate curves, invite glare, engineer velocity)

One idea was, What would Frankie see? How would he react? Would Frankie on the road be restless or deliberate? With a ballpoint I wrote L-O-V-E on the knuckles of my left hand and H-A-T-E on the right, but it wasn't the answer. Eye-level compositions were not the answer. Should I try not to focus at all?

Increasingly, my sensible Datsun was an embarrassment, a timid signature. Frankie would drive some kind of muscle car with tachometer, Frenched headlights, a hood scoop. I pictured an expanse of tailfin in thirty coats of hand-rubbed candy-apple red. I thought of the acute angle as an abstraction of speed, thrust, dynamism. What is it to understand a language and still not be able to speak it?

ALBERT FRANCONA

AKA "FRANKIE"
White Male
Age: 29
Height: 5′ 10″
Weight: 160
Color of Eyes: Black
Color of Hair: Black

SUBJECT IS WANTED IN CONNECTION WITH SERIES OF AGGRAVATED SEXUAL ASSAULTS IN NEW ENGLAND AND MID-ATLANTIC STATES. KNOWN TO FREQUENT PHOTO STUDIOS, GREASE PITS, BOWL-A-RAMAS. SCORNS FIREARMS, BUT SHOULD BE CONSIDERED EXTREMELY DANGEROUS.

It takes vigilance not to succumb to the numbers—f-stops, motel rates, highway designations, diner checks, exposure times—and one is not always up to it. The odometer turning to 50,000 becomes an anticipated Event. The glove compartment fills up with receipts, a wealth of documentation. Billboards and license plates turn unpreventably into algebra. A certain fecklessness sets in. And then a certain tension, which can be relieved only by sight of time and temperature specified in filament bulb mosaic on the rotating sign in front of a small-town bank.

Awareness deluges when not modulated, when not finely tuned. It can become a kind of panic.

Expenditure: $62.31
1738 miles @ 26 mpg
67 gals. gas @ avg. price 93 cents

Stella, legally, should be starting school, but my wife and I are loath to part with her. Is this a lack of faith in institutions, or something more selfish? Either way, it probably is natural for members of the overeducated class. Daphne's mother cannot say often enough that her daughter is "too clever by half." In my own case, form follows function until exhausted but never catches up. A rerun in every direction, I mean. Stella announces: "Chocolate is fabulous." Daphne has on Verdi or Bizet, and Stella shudders, yells, "I hate this music!" She has something to say with these words; they are not merely thrown up like tinsel onto a tree. We cherish in her such certainties, such firm insistence, and are loath to see them replaced by anxiety, ambivalence, embarrassment, retreat—what, in short, seem to be the necessary perversions.

ROADWAY VERNACULAR
(A Preliminary Syllabus)

Baines, Melissa, *Urban Motif Congestion,* Argon Press, West Covina, 1979.

De Marco, H. D., *Rest and Respite: From Caravanseri to Truckstop*, printed privately, 1968.

McMahon, T. K., *Looking at the World Through a Windshield,* HomeRun Books, San Francisco, 1981.

Niemann, Dieter, *Phänomenologie des Autobahns*, Kultur Zeitung, Bern, 1977.

Platt, David Alan, *Neon Democracy,* Dreyfuss-
   Peterkin, Boston, 1983.
Traven, Bob, *First with the Best: A History of U.S. 1,*
   Tire & Rubber Institute, Akron, 1965.

"Don't get too wrapped up," said nearly everyone who knew about my project. "Drive safely."

I carried in the trunk of my car a first-aid kit, jumper cables, flares, a heavy-duty flashlight, kept my thermos filled with coffee, was careful to husband my energies and stay alert. Still, as it turned out, the dice weren't sufficiently loaded.

I remember a distinct but unnameable shift of light, hard impact, raining glass, and then a kind of torpid, nauseous remove that was almost like snobbery. "Oh, just relax," I might have said. Or, "Call the roller of big cigars." I remember a texture of white clamshell, surf hissing around my ears. And O'Hara, unmarked and unfazed, the prick, his Dodge half-ton barely scraped, O'Hara making a cozy offer, his arm around me, snuff-stained teeth and rapid blinking.

In the taxi, I came more to myself, lenses spread out around me on the seat. Blue sea and blue sky seemed to roll as one. Just the note, I thought, to fill and then combine the chord. Go on. Make friends with it.

I sold the car and flew home.

DAY OF ACCIDENT	*May 18, 1986*
TIME OF DAY	*10:15 a.m.*
WEATHER	*Clear*
LIGHT CONDITION	*Daylight*
ROAD SURFACE	*Dry*

OCCURRED ON
(Name St., Rd. or Rte. #)   *U.S. 1*
AT INTERSECTION WITH
(Name St., Rd. or Rte. #)   *Dade Co. 905*
CITY NAME
(Or Nearest City)   *Key Largo*

I look over the four contact sheets while they are still wet, am pleased right off to see a balance of formal and informal, a mixture of broad long-shot and close-in detail. I pour out another glass of Old Overholt, straight rye whiskey bottled in Cincinnati, and, along with my big-band tapes, a habitual darkroom accoutrement. True, I like certain things to be just so, but who cares any more about workmanship? These are bits, blips, snippets, and not as careful as they look. Starting anywhere. Taking the last sheet, reading the rightmost negative strip, which on its upper edge says KODAK SAFETY FILM 5063, and on its lower edge names exposures 16 through 21.

—paired gas pumps, rectangular digital display units topped with identical PAY FIRST signboards
—old man forcing smile in motel breezeway, NAPA cap, bill stained
—industrial exhaust stacks, low angle
—church steeple paralleled by traffic light stanchion
—self-portrait behind the wheel (camera held at arm's length), visible fatigue, characteristic alternation of aimless and frantic
—family group at Tastee Freez picnic table, night (flash fill)

Mom, dad, two girls, one boy. "We're a service family." Contemplative dad sipping thick shake. "MacDill AFB, Tampa. Antiaircraft. It's all computers now." Taking their latest transfer in stride, fatalists. "Work's always there, so you follow it." I had to envy resignation chosen and not settled for. Watched them roll slowly away in a camper lashed with luggage and bikes.

This is "Prelude to a Kiss." Benny Carter's 1942 band, very mellow reeds. And these still are only scraps, chips, slivers. That they can be fixed in a coherent sum is the kind of stance we live on, like entropy or antimatter: pretty fictions that don't explain, furtive agreements of pretense, a wink and a ducking away.

Modulate.

Modulate. All right.

But I can't stop wanting to know what I'm looking at.

FINDING FLORIDA

Che and an old friend, Alberto Granados, launched on a prolonged tour of Latin America by motorcycle and on foot at the end of 1951 . . . Chile via Patagonia . . . Peru . . . the Amazon . . . Colombia . . . Venezuela . . . Granados stayed in Venezuela and Guevara, travelling in a plane loaded with thoroughbred horses, spent a month in Miami.

RICHARD BOURNE
Political Leaders of Latin America

●

R U M B L I N G 12,000 feet above the Caribbean: The cargo hold was frigid, and Che, wheezing, heated water for maté with an immersion coil.

"They don't agree with you, the horses?" asked Placido, the groom.

"Asthma," Che explained.

Supported by canvas belly slings, the nervous animals

quivered in their stalls, breathing in short bursts. Placido soothed them, humming, rubbing, adjusting leg pads. Sucking the maté little by little, like his grandmother, Che thought of Racetrack and Soccer Field as two political parties: pomp and control versus tumult and passion.

In Leticia, where the borders of Brazil, Peru, and Colombia converge, Granados had been hired to coach a junior soccer team. Most of the players went barefoot, and their only ball leaked air. But they were tireless, ferocious tacklers, and ran all day with no more fuel than coffee and bread.

The plane shuddered in an air pocket, and Placido sprang up, throwing his arms around a colt's neck. Che thought: He works for the horses, not for the boss.

———

I N Miami, at the airport luncheonette, Che had a doughnut and three glasses of water. Behind the counter, on a mat of paper grass, was a baby alligator, stuffed, with an orange in its jaws. He did not understand the money or the language. What kind of penance was this? New contexts for study, every form of contradiction. United Snakes, Granados called it. Really, the trip was already over. Proven: He could act on impulse like anyone else, Ernesto, the methodical future physician. Evident: He should have stayed in Caracas.

Che approached a man in an authoritative black visor cap to ask about hotels.

"Sure, you want a place talks your talk, serves your food. Come on, my cab's right outside."

In the wide car Che heard American radio for the first

time, brass music, an overexcited voice. He thought of Evita when she was on the radio. "Brought to you by Jabon Radical." Evita as Lucrezia Borgia. Evita as Joan of Arc . . . Evita dying now in Buenos Aires, but giving her alms to the end, to the unending line of supplicants, her descamisados, moving toward the marble hall on Avenida Real.

"Hey," the cabbie said. "Are you in the cigar business?"

The Moncada desk clerk didn't care to see his passport, just cash in advance. The room had a sink, but no toilet. The bedspread was edged with dangling pom-poms of chenille. From the window he could see the backs of several buildings, a Chinese cook smoking by the trash cans.

Later he sat on a green couch in the deserted lobby and read Martí. He could smell seepage, mildew, some disagreeable cologne. He leafed through tattered magazines and saw slogans like "Safety-Flow Ride" and "Self-Cleaning Magic." Two prostitutes came in, noticed his rope sandals, and went right by. Che smoked his pipe and went to bed hungry.

———

C H E knew where he was in the morning: alone with not enough money. He had guava and cream cheese for breakfast. He brewed maté in his room and studied a map. The ocean was miles away.

A postcard (Everglades 'Gator Wrestling) to friends:

Dear Hawkeye & Tonio—Greetings from another onetime Spanish possession. But nobody worries about History here. Everything is paved. When the sun doesn't shine, they give a refund. The local air seems to help my asthma. Back soon for exams? Maybe.

Love to all—Nesto

He went outside to look for stamps, walked quite a way not finding any. Nearly everyone he saw wore a hat. Their faces, even while smiling, were preoccupied, expectant. Heat came up as he went. There were scarred trees. Dogs ran loose and idlers smashed bottles. An aroma of scorched snack-bar onions passed on the air. Women in white shoes bargained with a man selling fish from the trunk of his car, boys jeered and shadow-boxed—everyone was black. A man in chauffeur's whipcords stood by himself at the end of the street. He kept looking up, scanning, as though waiting for a bomber group to appear.

——

O N E morning the manager of the hotel brought coffee straight to his room.

"Black as the devil, hot as hell and sweet as love," she said.

Celia carried her wealth on her body, like a gypsy. There were rings on every finger. Che was embarrassed.

"Argentina, eh? You look like a gaucho."

"I'm from Buenos. My family is in the shipping business."

"You got the smarts, all right. I'm not so old so I don't notice."

It was hard to find Celia's real age under so much rouge

and rice powder. She'd come here just after the war, she said, from Havana, where she'd been a beautician and a santeria priestess.

"Here some busboy wants to turn his sweetheart. I sweep the place, I cut the chicken, pour the rum, but no loa comes. Ogun won't talk. Shango won't talk. Nothing. I find out you got to do for yourself here. Nobody else going to."

Celia was sitting on the edge of the bed now. She squeezed his hand.

"But I like you. What I'm thinking, I could help you get a camera, make you a business. Like at the fronton, the dog track, and the zoo. Also parks and outside nightclubs. Turistas have to prove they been. They pay for you to take picture."

"I don't need work," Che said, lighting his pipe. "Just coffee."

———

YESTERDAY'S newspaper had announced a sixteenth straight day of sunshine, but today it stormed. Che ducked into an arcade. He saw his reflection in the window of a luggage shop, wide-eyed, unshaven, confused. He could not help looking over his shoulder. In Toffenetti's—Haberdashery for Men, he browsed until ejected by clerks. He ate a small bag of peanuts. The clock over the newsreel-theater box office was encircled by a flickering blue neon tube. Che was tempted to think that measurement, the language of numbers, was another form of hearsay—he was an uncomfortable materialist. But he knew that six hydrogen atoms in a ring with six of chlorine made Gammexane. That intangibly slow summer between terms he had developed the insecticide in his father's garage, tested it on river mosquitoes in Zárate. His father, tangibly, had offered the capital necessary for small-scale manufacture.

He took a seat in the back row of the theater. The travelogue was about Indonesia. It showed elephants at work in a teak forest. After that came an instructional film on home canning. Che studied the backs of heads, diagnosing impatience and inertia both. Phrenology in the dark, and onscreen the graduated dial of a pressure cooker.

"Here the string beans are processed in steam for at least twelve minutes to insure that any spores of *Clostridium botulinum* are destroyed."

Che went into the men's. He washed, avoiding himself in the mirror, filled and tamped his pipe, saw the feet sticking out. They were battered and bruised, shoeless. He opened the stall door. A tramp lay curled among newspaper, his head alongside the base of the toilet, one eye crusted over.

"Are you ill, señor? Let me help."

The tramp covered himself with papers. "Beat it. Piss off."

Che watched an unruly black duck blab its way out of the roasting pan in a color cartoon. He thought of microbes swarming invisibly over the floor.

———

L O O K I N G for a post office so he could wire home for money, Che found a library instead. Granite gray, pillared, dense, it was dustily cool inside, while petunias planted round the flagpole wilted in the heat. The shelves were brown and thick with varnish. The ceiling fans were still. He pulled a book at random—*A Bride in the Hand* by Lila Claire (C)—and caught a falling ant that had been laying its eggs inside, or eating the glue.

The librarian's freckled elbows supported her at the desk. She had a thin nose, red hair fine as a baby's, and was lovely in her sleepiness. Just over her shoulder, in light that leaked under the shade, particles of dust barely moved. And Che, struck by desire sudden and acute as asthma, could not move at all. She was Lila to him, a flight. He would turn the other people in the room to paper. He would shrink the room itself. And his hand would fit hers so easily, an afterthought.

He understood murder: When the thing you want most but cannot have is so close that it overflows the eye.

———

C E L I A told his fortune with cards. She showed him the queen of hearts and said he would die for love. Che was embarrassed.

"Better than dying by accident," she said.

He remembered the first corpse he had ever seen, remembered incoherent sensings in the way that dream pieces return, so vividly that they must actually have happened. It was just spring, the park pale green with buds, walking home and the school satchel chafing his leg. She lay under a tree, a pine tree, not old or young, gray as a clam, bewildered, and none of the men standing around had thought to close her eyes.

"You shouldn't think so much," Celia said, refilling his cup.

"And what instead?"

Her smile made him think of incisions; there was lipstick on her teeth.

"Tell me. What instead?"

They were sitting at a square, oilcloth-covered table in the hotel kitchen, where everything was freshly stacked and wiped. It was late; even the wash boy had left. Celia had Havana tuned in on the radio, Arsenio Rodriguez, a mambo. She cut the deck twice without looking: Jack of spades, jack of spades.

"Go ahead. Don't make yourself a choice."

The time he truly wanted to be a doctor, writing out twenty-five reasons. When had that been? He could see her red nails on the back of his hand, but the flesh was numb.

He recalled a line from Martí: "That which is suspicion today will be outcry tomorrow."

——

T H E bus had been loud with arguing. The beach was crowded, but quiet. Che rolled up his trousers and waded. He found green bits of glass tumbled smooth, a jellyfish big as a hubcap. With each receding wave needle-billed birds ran up to peck at airholes in the sand.

He thought of Granados swinging a gaviota to break its neck, and the foul meat they swallowed to show they were ready for anything. The "wastes" of Patagonia: Just starting out, full of dare, they had burned all their guidebooks and maps in the cookfire. Sand in the gas tank, sand on the chain sprockets, while the beach was covered with clicking black stones. And they talked all night about the great Italian restaurants in Santiago.

Che understood that they wanted him to take their picture. Overelaborate mime. Hold it this way, press down here. The man got between the two women, his arms draped over them, theirs circling his waist.

"Más. Uno más!"

Then he had to get between the women. They smelled of oranges. He knew his ribs stuck out and he needed a bath. The

man said something. Che shrugged. The man gave him a warm
can of beer and went away.

The "wilds" of Amazonas, the "rugged peaks" of Peru.
Miami Beach Welcomes You. The Playground Paradise. Everyone, he supposed, carried a guidebook, a catalogue of expecta-
tions which made it possible to travel without going anywhere,
to go nowhere while traveling. Only the sea, he supposed, was
without borders.

> A postcard (Avenue of Palms) home:
> Dear Family,
> I am well. This is not a ransom note. Trust that
> there is some explanation for my being here, and as
> soon as I know what it is, you will too. When Ponce
> de León searched for his fountain, anything seemed
> possible by the method of wandering. For today the
> only result is fatigue.
>
> Love to all—E.G.

He could not risk Celia's charity any longer. The organ
stings of bad drama were all too easy to imagine. He noticed
the smell of church incense in her vicinity. He found candy
on his pillow, and now even the maids called him "gaucho."
But then he had come to mistrust his own judgment. Mundane
objects seemed to impose themselves, mundane words took on
too many meanings. "Something in the water" was his grandmother's expression, applied to any distress. Was it absurd to
wonder if Celia was drugging the coffee? The more he tried
to clear his head, the worse the tangle became. United Snakes.
Wriggling in the water.

This was the time, a typically reticent Sunday. Celia's

cockatiel was swooping around the lobby as he went out. The cars on the boulevard were shiny. He passed a cotton candy wagon and a blue drugstore. The expansion of his lungs made him smile.

If he made his route back a straight line, there were a hundred islands in between, lagoons and melon juice and coral heads and fast deadly fish. He passed a boy selling coconuts with painted faces. He supposed an island boy like that who could say: "El Señor? He lived all those years in a place behind that hill, and no one ever knew a thing about him."

If you knew how, there was true satisfaction in being tired. He had his duffel bag, and a brim above his eyes, and he was walking south.

No Smoking

●

J o a n was having a birthday the way other people have flu. She'd turned thirty-seven five days ago, but those forlorn and morbid symptoms still hung on. The ferries tripled on Friday and everyone already on the island took deep breaths. She passed the scone shop and the book nook and the toggery. She passed Ramona's sidewalk tables, where trust-fund carpenters sat with their imported ale. They wore jaunty little hats. They discussed timber prices and dilemmas of wiring. The dogs at their feet were stuporously pictorial.

She'd got up on her birthday (sunny after early-morning fog) believing that in some way she must mark it. One evaded or ignored a charged event and its tendency was to curve back with months of trouble. Nothing convinced her. But she had rules for safety, remote, uncodified. She put a half pint of Jim Beam in her pocket and went all over the beach thinking how plain she was in every way. She hunkered by tide pools, chanting in her mental voice, "I will never never have children." Vapid abjections, indulgent. As a punishment, she stopped smoking.

A man stepped around her in the post office, a man wearing, with no sense of parody, Top Siders, tomato-juice pants, and a crocodile sport shirt.

"So what the hell are you on?" he said.

People waited in line who were not accustomed to waiting in line. They held claim slips for products they had bought by mail: country curtains, language tapes, barometers, bird-of-prey lithographs, authentic Creole pralines.

She took her change into the wooden booth. Eight rings, a gulped hello, her brother-in-law sounding unhappily startled by her voice.

"Richard, I walked in four miles to make this call."

"Everything's all right?"

"I wanted to talk. I mean, I do want to."

"Randi isn't here. She's driving the kid up to allergy camp."

"Right."

"Are you very tired? You sound tired."

"I stopped cigarettes."

"You're a tough kid."

"So where are you going to be middle of next week?"

"No telling." Always in his voice that apologetic little shrug. "I've never seen the Vineyard."

She wanted to say something astonishing and intimate. A different conversation spilled onto their line, then tumbling relays. She heard him swallow.

The sandals dangled from her hand now, leather blackened by sweat, hieroglyphically dappled. There were tar bubbles in the road and she popped them. The air vibrated from motors all around the island: scooters, chain saws, a backhoe. She smelled pine instead of the sea. Hardened gum, no weed or salt. Insects instead of fish. Foliage painted on mailboxes dismayed her. Flamenco guitar swirled from a patio. In the sky there were no clouds, no art director's arrangement. And what she wished was that she and Richard could be like a paperback French novel with a translucent stain of suntan oil on the opening page. The cheapest of bittersweet, but lasting.

Molly's car was not in the driveway, which meant she'd been sober enough to find the keys. Molly's great-grandfather found silver in Nevada. Her first two husbands were developers. The last had been a member of the Danish royal family. So Joan lived in the back cottage for no rent—Molly could afford that. She kept the vegetable garden, fed the dogs, and most important, was in nights, just close enough to keep Molly from blowing her brains out.

I don't need work, just a name for it.

This also was in her mental voice, the one that spoke several dialects.

A drizzly almost-evening washed off the last of the "set" colors. She sat outside smelling of insect repellent and tried to think of some reason to now be in love with her sister's husband. Randi, her youngest, most reliably conventional sister, and Richard with his professional eyes. It was not a situation that lent itself comfortably to "thought." She looked back at the cottage, orange candle glow behind the two tiny windows. It was a box, silvery weathered shakes and green trim. It was a box that might as easily be for storing floating booms and cranberry flats as for living in. She had been in it almost three years.

Twelve birthdays ago, a round number, she had been in Denver earning a quite alarming salary as editor of a sportswear company's in-house magazine. She drove a Saab, lived in a rental "chalet," owned recreational equipment. But she found being complacent extremely hard work. Anyway, that was how she put it in her mental voice. Perhaps it was very much more a matter of her inability to make, or rather to keep, friends. How quickly she began to notice the triviality of others, their repetitious bluff, childish calculation. Was she insightful or only petty?

"Have you seen Puck?" Molly asked, describing a slight arc across the lawn, like a rightward-breaking putt.

"Not since this morning."

Puck was the basset hound.

"Poor thing. I'm always afraid he'll forget where he lives."

Molly blew into her hands as though it were autumn. Poor Molly. She looked like the poster for an organization campaigning against the long-term danger of cosmetics.

"You went somewhere today? I saw the car was gone."

"Over to Gay Head. Isn't that an absolutely wonderful name? Yes, I went over to Gay Head to see about a catamaran that was advertised in the paper."

No, she wouldn't take the bait, wouldn't ask what possible use Molly, who hated water like a cat, could have for that fancy boat. Her landlady with the twelve-foot sofa and the ginger-jar lamps, but no telephone; because of one disputed bill, Molly denied herself the lonesome drunk's most precious outlet.

She admired the reality, not the principle, said now, "Animals are brave because they're stupid."

"I know just what you mean," Molly said, not elaborating.

That night just before sleep, purely as an exercise, she imagined Richard with the body of a woman.

On Sunday, as usual, she was late to the church and sat

in back. The sermon took as its text an obscure verse from the book of Micah, and followed a confusing line. But when the organ played "A Mighty Fortress Is Our God," though it sounded out of joint and driven by steam, she was moved to tears.

By two o'clock the sun had burned through the haze and she put on a bathing suit to work in the garden. She pulled green worms pin-striped with yellow off the broccoli and dropped them in a tin of kerosene. She weeded and staked, cut beet tops for soup. And all the time she was dying for a cigarette.

Twenty-nine birthdays ago (as it turned out, all of these numbers were round), having unequivocally refused to go with her family on their two-week trip to Lake Champlain, she was staying on 138th Street with her baby-sitter, whose given name in full was Jimmie C. Glass. Jimmie's husband, Hubert, came from Barbados and worked as an elevator operator at the Hotel Theresa. Hubert told her animal stories that always had a moral at the end. Jimmie sat in the kitchen, the same as she did downtown, adding long columns of figures on the backs and fronts of envelopes; and she showed in the *Daily News* how the last three digits in the mutuel handle at Belmont Park made the magic number. On the birthday they took her to a big cafeteria on St. Nicholas Avenue and let her eat nothing but dessert. Later they all put on foil hats and listened to Hubert's rumba albums.

On Monday she wrote a letter to Randi full of hallowed family anecdotes and quotations from Stendhal, put a dollar's worth of stamps on the plain white envelope, and mailed it to an imaginary street in Cagayan de Oro on the Philippine island of Mindanao.

Puck was still absent. Molly wandered the neighborhood all morning with a box of Milk-Bone, calling the dog's name as loudly as she could, and was predictably misunderstood by a home owner, who called the Vineyard Haven constables. Molly was abusive in the cruiser and arrived home in cuffs.

After putting Molly to bed, convincing her to take a little soup, she went to the cottage to knit. There were shops on the island that paid her as much as seventy-five dollars a sweater. The needle rhythm, which usually calmed her, now had no effect, and she worried more and more over Richard. The alpaca yarn felt unpleasant against her skin, like moth wings. She undressed, lay down on the bunk, and tried to see her body as Richard would, as a question resolved. She liked the hair on her legs, but would he? Should she shave?

Aloud, in her regular voice, she said, "This could be a decision."

That night, unable to sleep, she thought of her mother's legendary knitting. With great care and the aid of graph paper, seated at the kitchen table like Jimmie, chain-smoking, her mother would plot out figures for the family sweaters: reindeer, castle turrets, leaping salmon, Mahler full-face. The skin was brown and taut over her hands.

Before dawn on Wednesday she applied toenail polish called Creme Coral. She knew that Richard admired her feet. Once after a badminton game, with Randi inside making gazpacho, he'd held them and said they felt like little animals. She picked a light-green sleeveless dress that fell below her shins and sunglasses with thick black frames. It didn't matter. Richard's professional eyes would only see what they wanted to.

She began the walk, feeling more and more frightened, tighter and tighter in her stomach. She refused rides from a dental assistant in white acetate, two men on the way to golf, and shivered in the damp. Queen Anne's lace grew thick and high at the edge of the road, and smelled like poison carrots. To her left, following their own road through sumac and scrub oak, power lines crackled. After an hour, cold and sick, she rested on a warm asphalt driveway. Close at hand were dead, dry things that looked smokable. Probably, she thought, it would be wise to spend the day here.

Richard's car trundled off the ferry. She saw his face—dark, drawn, uncertain—before he was able to prepare it, and felt comforted. He kissed her like a brother-in-law, spoke her name like a movie lover. They went to Ramona's for cappuccino. Richard looked at his watch.

"What did you tell her?" she said.

"About a tropical medicine seminar in New Haven."

"Did she believe you?"

"In her way. Don't worry. It wouldn't matter if she knew."

"Does that mean you'll tell?" She scraped angrily at dried foam inside her cup.

"Tell what?" He touched her face. "Erase all that. It's just you and me now."

That was the right thing to say, even the right way to say it. But her head was thick with the flu of her birthday. And her little sister, his wife, was the whole point. Yes? Her mental voice had a sore throat.

"Do you know how old I am?" she said.

"More or less."

He stroked the back of her neck. They drove on dirt roads. She fingered the amber worry beads that dangled from the mirror.

"Would you like to swim?" she said, meaning, Can we take our clothes off now?

He answered by slapping in a Fats Waller tape. She remembered the winter Randi had won a scholarship competition, playing something slow and Slavic, wearing a popcorn-stitch sweater from Mother. She remembered the summer Randi went to study in Munich. Fats Waller sang about two sleepy people much too in love to say goodnight.

"You have beautiful ears," Richard said.

But he did not stop the car.

As a punishment, they would have dinner with Molly that night and get very drunk. Richard and Molly would go upstairs. She would walk by herself on the cold, plain, moonlit beach. In the tide pools there will be starfish she will pick up and put back. Her footprints will be phosphorescent. She will climb back up the path and stand in wet grass outside her cabin until she can make herself go in.

Joan's mental voice tired itself with such stories as they drove through the dust and were thirsty.

COWS ON THE
DRAG STRIP

●

L ARVELL stepped from morning glare into the climate-
controlled lobby. He had shaved in the car with his portable
electric. This was his first appointment of the day. He was
scheduled to meet with the operations manager to discuss how
a new plant security system might or might not affect their
liability coverage. A tall secretary with frosted hair escorted
him from reception to the elevators, and then through the
seventh-floor office wing.

"Have a seat." She smiled insincerely. Her teeth probably
were capped. "Mr. Koplik will be with you shortly."

Larvell brought his knees together and placed the Sam-
sonite briefcase across them. The material covering his chair
was unpleasant, slithy. It was 10:12 by the digital clock.

"Sorry you had to wait." Koplik rubbed his hands together too vigorously. "I was on long-distance."

Koplik's tie was a petroleum derivative. So was the
Atlanta Falcons beverage mug on his desk.

Larvell hummed Proverbs 13:5—The righteous hate what
is false—but it wasn't helping.

The file tabs were red, blue, yellow.

"I thought we should review," Larvell said.

Koplik was chewing gum. Very unprofessional.

"The terms of your policy," Larvell said.

Here came static, while his own voice seemed to drift. Here came clammy bursts, and pulsing like a hose of blood around his head.

Koplik was leaning down toward him and holding a hand out.

———

BEING rigorous and thoughtful, you could probably trace it way, way back. But the real trouble, the trouble that got in every waking minute and wouldn't leave, had begun on Wednesday when he stopped for lunch at a Chuck's Wagon outside Tuscaloosa. It was crowded, so he had to sit at the counter. He ordered white coffee and a French Dip, and the girl thanked him for his order, smiling. He pictured a great big steamboat roast with rosy meat puckering up under the serrations of a carving knife, and juice running down all golden with the essence of beef. Then he saw the girl tear open a foil packet and pour what was in it into the gravy dish. When Larvell saw the girl making his au jus from hot water and brown dust out of a packet, it was a message. It was a powerful message, a revelation of the bogus, the false, the synthetic. It overwhelmed him inside, a movement of spirit. It was like the Spirit of the Living God giving him as though never before eyes to see with and ears to hear, and the power to understand what he saw and what he heard. So Larvell knew there resided no more truth in the men around him than in their simulated rawhide wallets, drip-dry shirts, deodorant insoles, no more than in the plastic cactus of the room where they came to brag and sell. The pretend-posed-as-the-real was everywhere. Each new revelation of the revelation fell like a blow. Larvell was stunned, could barely keep his feet. He wanted to get in his car and just sit. But there was velour upholstery posing as velvet, and synthetic pine fragrance from a green cardboard tree on the dash. Larvell prayed as he drove and he prayed in his room at the Travelodge off I-59. He read in Joshua (Be strong and of a good courage; be not afraid, neither be dismayed: for the Lord is with you wheresoever you go), and in Revelations (So, because you are lukewarm—neither hot nor cold—I am about to spit you out of my mouth). He asked God how he might come to wisdom through this understanding of synthetics. He asked for guidance. In the morning Larvell telephoned his wife. She had the radio on, a call-in show, and he told her to turn it down. He heard the practice in her voice, the effort of interest in what town he was calling from, which town he'd been in the day before, and which he was heading for now. Larvell tried to describe how it felt receiving the message, but somewhere between formation in his mind and execution by his mouth, the words fell apart. She said if he was about to go all Pentecostal at this hour, just forget it. He said that what he had now was like X-ray vision. She said Holly was out on the porch with her Froot Loops, and hold on while I get her. Larvell saw the hollow aluminum portico in front of his house. He saw his daughter in the swing seat, gazing at a smear of lipstick on her spoon, saw her running shoes come down on the green all-weather carpet meant to look like grass, and he hung up. For the rest of that day, and into the next, Larvell tried to will normalcy; that is, he tried to ignore all the confirmations. Like tanning salons. Like gas station dinosaurs, and billboards that said Home Cookin'! Like elevator music. He had a Saturday golf date with a Memphis friend, but didn't go. Instead, he crossed over to Arkansas, into the piney woods. He got egg sandwiches and Nestea from a store, and pulled off at a cut in the road where a little stream ran and there were picnic tables. It was a dry, humming heat. He rolled up his sleeves, saw his arms all flabby and white. The eggs were salty and the bread soft. He tried listening to a Jimmy Swaggart sermon-on-tape (For it says no sin. It doesn't say just a little bit; it says no sin shall enter there. Not even a hint), but it was too dramatized, too much for effect. It was a high sky; he went in the trees to get away from it. The dry mat of needles was springy underfoot. He could remember what it was like at nine years old back in Monterey, following jaybirds into a thicket. Here it was clear light just ahead, and a hissing sprinkler. Larvell counted eight house lots, three up for sale. He walked back to his car. There was a black lace bra in the trash. He got caught in the glare and push of afternoon traffic. All around him were these men surging, braking, clenching their jaws, with no recognition of what they were angry about. He saw the dealer license plate frames. Mel Brady Pontiac. Vince Farr Subaru. He saw a bumper sticker that said God Has Numbered Every Hair On Your Head . . . And On Your Wig, Too. That night Larvell got in a fight at the salad bar of the Airport Circle Inn. He was stopped dead there by the fake bacon bits made out of soy when this big moke goes, move it, bud, and raps him on the back of the hand with a dressing ladle. He sank a left hook under the moke's liver and then they were rolling around on the floor with croutons in their hair. Larvell got put in holding with a skinny black kid in a torn rayon shirt, light blue with big white orchids. This kid had a thin smile. Cracker, he said, you don't like me fifty-one ways from the ace of spades. It was Sunday, His day, when a guard came down to say there weren't going to be any charges, and Larvell should get his ass out of town while it was still attached.

———

KOPLIK wrung out the handkerchief, wrapped it around fresh ice, and returned it.

"Your color's coming back," he said.

The tall secretary with the gray streak dividing her bangs was right behind, bent in some unfinished gesture.

"I'm sorry," Larvell said. "I don't want to make trouble."

"God, don't apologize."

Koplik squeezed Larvell's shoulder; the girl straightened up, nodding.

"Hey, the stress thing. We all know what that's like. Sure, aim high, eye on the prize. But then you get all wired in and you're running around like an insect." Koplik drew up his mouth at the corners. "Where's the payoff?"

"With me it's a caffeine addiction." That big girl was still nodding. "And also refined sugars."

Koplik fingered his inside pocket. "Don't apologize. Really."

"I'm going for acupuncture," the girl said.

Larvell got up to go. He had the beige sport coat over his arm like a robber concealing a gun. He declined the taxi Koplik was insistent on phoning for. The outside air was heavy and thick, and it didn't have to sneak up behind you.

Here was the company logo in brushed chrome on a black marble slab, and then all this lawn with rollings built in, and thin trees put down like game markers.

————

D R I V I N G till sunset, then sleeping jackknifed on the back seat until dawn. Crossing over the big river at Vicksburg, going down through Madison Parish, Lake Bruin, Waterproof, Cocodrie. It seemed important to have honest clothes—cotton T-shirt, denim pants, canvas shoes—and to throw the old things away. Slowing down along the blacktop to recognize that planing mill with its rust-sprung roof fallen in, Haney's tar-papered barbecue place, the Pig Stand, and the four elms where you turned off to go midnight swimming. Larvell stopped the car and he could hear the underbrush whisper. This had all been Gannet land, leased for cotton from the Texas & Pacific. Junior Gannet shot up his leg hunting snipe from a horse. Lee Leon Gannet gave him the Esso station to run. It went from squinting weather into haze. The road stayed empty. They'd made a catchment and put in a boat ramp for sportsmen. Before, the land made a natural levee reinforced by trees. Each man would have his trees flagged, and he owned those trap lines, going out through mist after a cool night to pull his wire traps up out of the mud, shake the crawdads out, bait them back up with chicken guts. The road had a few sail-rabbits, which meant any creature squashed flat and dried hard enough to pick up and skim through the air. Right across from where Larvell ran out of gas, let the car half skew down a kudzu bank, was the spot where Cal Stark and his big brother wanted to build the Monterey Assembly of God Church.

Ground's too soft, and too far out in the woods, Lee Leon said, and it was his money. Cal Stark had a little fifteen-minute morning radio show on WNTZ sponsored by Bluebelle Vanilla Wafers. He sang a Jim Reeves ballad, gave the weather, did something uptempo with flat-picking, read an item of human interest from the news, always finished with a hymn. Cal finally married Gail Fullham, who played piano in the cinder-block church her uncle went and put up right in town. She answered every altar call, and spoke in the unknown tongues. Larvell came down two years ago when Orris Mitchell got married to a Fullham cousin—he and Mitch had run around Houston together when they were young, worked construction, sold used cars. Mitch told how on the far bank of the Tensas, up by Ray's Bluff, cows would get loose and wander over on the drag strip that had gone in there like they had an old memory passed down in the blood. Because Wimp Gannet pasturing out there took you way, way back. Lee Haney ran his still about that same time, a fifty-gallon unit in a cave back under the bluff, and they'd be in there tending the firebox, tapping the petcock, eating side meat and corn fritters from a black iron skillet. Lee had Choctaw blood. Bit off a treasury man's nose, died in prison. Airborne seed fluff went by. Someone tended the footpath. Larvell, mounting to the little cemetery in the trees, said something under his breath.

BUDDED ON EARTH TO BLOOM IN HEAVEN

Baby Langston, just two, from croup. The limestone marker with a lamb carved in. Weeds pulled and leaf trash swept by. Higher ground. Solid ground and plain truth. My kinsmen have gone away. Aunt Lucille never played cards or went to a movie, said a woman shouldn't smell but of lye soap.

1891–1965
PEACE AT LAST IN HIS ARMS

Moss in the pipe rail joints, geraniums wilting in a big tomato can. Gannet land, red dirt. Pop dug up an arrow point and said it was Indian mounds. Wagging his finger, learn to follow your trail through life without leaving one. Be tested, be brave. Clipping from the Beaumont paper on a derrick fire victim named Roy Moore, 53. She said it might be another one, not our Roy. Scolding the molasses on her greens, the sugar diabetes and the blubber on her hips. A continuous test of faith. Set a crucible in the fire, and let it be a refining fire. Cut amber beads on her dresser. Satin pillows and a mansion on the hill.

WILMETTE JUNE GANNET MOORE
LOVING MEMORIES

Larvell said something under his breath.

A Tale of
No More Demands

●

U N A V O I D A B L Y , always, humming spiders and iridescent lichen brought notice of spring to the domain. A great sigh, and the people said, well, of course, yes, again. Off came the shutters, and the lids from the water troughs. Hedgerows were unlimbered from burlap. In the high unthawed meadows llamas agreed to prolonged sleep, and in warm blue inland lagoons the triggerfish were through practicing. At the palace, modest in size really, with its glass moat and untruculent sandstone battlements, modest for all to see—at his palace, François Rogelio IV, Emperor, puttered with chapel furnishings.

Delivered from the twenty-one interminable days of winter, he now could say, please, no more demands on my time. Tradition, unquestioned, though it lent discernible advantage to no one, made winter the season for petitioners and suplicants. Day and night they came—old men from the desert with performing horses, a firewalker, tumblers, women who told the future with nails, with dung, a farmer's boy who had glazed a microscopic likeness of Ilse, the Concubine, inside an almond shell—all desiring but his tiniest gesture of acknowledgment.

Interminable. Stinking tapers, mice in the blankets. And the shortage of fuel: trees unfelled and peat uncut. Sven, the Woodsman, was imprisoned. The dungeon was perfectly black, a place to think of larch and tamarack in acres, and the yield potential in planks. This worked for quite a while. It was just lately that Sven had lost his mind.

For contractions of the imperial stomach, its doggish growling, the twenty-first day and one at last brought relief: raw cockles and flatbread, which Françoise Rogelio ate dutifully, and without savor. The gold cutlery and damask cloth made him sad. They had come over trade routes which were forgotten in that diabolic one-day winter when honey turned to varnish, and husbands woke up strangers to their wives. Now clouds rolled by. Sea gulls miles from any sea roosted on the parapets.

Ilse was compelled by spring and in her velvets came to Rodolfo, the Confessor. And she knelt before him to say, Little Father, I have inflicted pain. I have corrupted children and had congress with animals and I have not repented. Rodolfo silently moved his lips, and the Concubine licked rock salt from his hand until her throat burned.

In a tiny lime-white cottage, Lenore, the Virgin, bent over her tatting, didn't see that sunlight had come in the window. Her slender perfect hands were careful at the work. She had a simple heart, never was troubled by expectation. At the time of the siege by heathen mercenaries, she had sealed both her cleft and her fundament with red wax and gone out to tend the wounded, the mad, the sick, and the dying. Bowmen dissembled their pain to fall in love with her, and running pus turned to milk.

Evening descended quickly, with click beetles at their posts, fumes of new dust on the air. The flock politely breathed together, formed rhomboids, pentagons. Zoltan, the Shepherd, did not know patience as a word or an idea, but he was replete at the end of the winter fast simply from watching worms move through a hunk of cheese. He fed his reed pipes into the fire piece by piece.

The ragged shape stumbling over bogs in a conflation of bell-chiming was Cassius, the Leper. Moonlight very much became him. He preened with despair, groping for edible mist. How could he live on integrity alone? But no one else had cared to design his banishment. Clear chiming amid the drift. He called out indictments to challenge the Emperor: Flaccid in the pose of strength, you have outlived your time. Resource-less! Unbegotten! Spayed!

Mating cavies filled the afternoon with spray and newts tumbled out of the trees. It was the second day of spring; from guano-spattered ramparts the disconsolate Emperor looked abroad. Where once there had been garden, roses to gather and tangerines to squeeze, there now was featureless meadow. Where there had been meadow on which to ride out hawking, there was a tangle of thornbush and stranglers. No more Animating Divinity in and of the earth, no more heroism, no will to overcome.

Possibly, things had not been disremembered, but only, as Rodolfo said, elided. And so the Emperor slept on a board while his Confessor made a bed of lavender and furs, brooded over a jug of moss water while the Little Father, sipping clove liqueur, played motets at the harmonium. And so Ilse was still unrepentant, raking her sleepless flesh with nuggets of bee varnish. But the route was lost. She could no more dream her frescoes of venery.

The Woodsman made history. Deranged, disarranged, he had never been more himself. He issued edicts, decrees. From the fountainhead of Sven! And the people shrugged, mumbled, obeyed. He minted coins with his profile on both sides. He stayed executions, bestowed lands and titles on deserving hermits. His shackles dissolved in rust. He went blind.

Spark struck tinder and caught. Cassius was no less entitled to spring appetite. The lampreys he had speared from the common sewer now were ready to be dangled in smoke. He hurled florid epithets at all the dead chefs of the land. Misanthropes! Fakirs! Let them poke in middens for their supper. And chase ghosts through long meat kitchens. The Leper hunkered down. Split skin, fat and smoke. Such aromas as approached fell back from the crater that had once been his nose.

The Emperor's last Queen had betrayed him, disgraced him with a pardon-seller, and was beheaded. Now his Concubine sat beside him in the chapel and they stared at the malachite-inlaid casket rumored to house the Queenly remains. Hadn't she been gutted, then packed with opals? (Or was it potatoes?) And what of the alley trade in bone amulets? Ilse whispered that he had every right to break the seal, and go ahead, don't wait. He took up her cool fingers and with them pressed shut his eyes.

Henceforward, all sins are venial. Was that the way Rodolfo said it?

Gathering blooms for a votive bouquet, Lenore saw the Shepherd as he came over the road with a lamb in his arms. And what a fine countenance, she told herself, such purity. Zoltan had for so long been asleep inside the smell of lanolin that he could not begin to understand the warm nuances through which passed the Virgin's gaze. All he could think of to do was to open the lamb's throat with his poniard, letting its blood into the chalkdust of the road as a kind of offering.

In the same dark library vault where the Confessor combed through enchiridions of prophecy, where, amid moth powder

and glue fragrance, Ilse refined her science with codices of
nerve expansion, mucosal viscosity, François Rogelio IV, the
last of his line, bowed over family chronicles and wept at the
loneliness of power. Under his hands the parchment was
stiffly rucked, its illuminations flaking. The old proverbs made
a deadly weight. At opposite ends of a fracture, a fissure, and
nothing to hand across.

Some petty villain mixed feathers into the hay and now
the Little Father's best stallion had foundered. This vexed him
quite as much as His Majesty's whimpers, not to say Ilse's pious
melancholia. Yes, he could see they were under compulsion—
like ants guarding larval packages under a rock—but this was
not a useful recognition. And what was he supposed to say,
take out and smash all the mirrors? Hazards, both of them, in
any palace. Not that Rodolfo necessarily liked eating alone, but
nobody else knew how to relish food. They saw the most
succulent curries as masking ground glass, the perfect blushing
fruit as a vehicle for parasites. So it was his part to play from
the great carved mahogany chair, to stretch forth his arm,
there there, kiss the ring, my child, partake of serenity. And
among all these demands on his patience, someone had found a
motive and murdered his favorite horse. Revenge was too small
a thing to stay for long in the Confessor's mind. Hoofbeats,
hoofbeats. He might go down into the village for a game of
dominoes. Perdition. He had only to stretch forth his arm.

The flock was long gone over the hill. Silver bubbles broke
behind the weir. Woodbine and dog rose neatly shared a single
trellis. The Virgin made a steamed pudding of blood and offal
of which, until she coaxed his hand around a spoon, Zoltan took
no more than he could admire with his eyes. She watched the
motion of his burly stalwart arms. This was a different kind of
grace. Not like her salad greens planted as radiant spokes from

the wellhead, or like afternoon sun on the flank of a pail. Better. Not so definite. Zoltan explained that he'd been sent out with the animals just as soon as he could walk. Seasons might follow seasons without his seeing anyone, and so, not even wanting to, he had taught himself to sing. Lenore described without a blush what she did each night to fall asleep. They wanted to tell each other everything, or at least as much as could be remembered.

Ilse had come far to reach the cave mouth, far enough that her naked legs were all cut up with nettles and sedge grass. The Leper vibrated. She asked for his invitation in such a sweet, warming voice. He said, do come in and sit right down there, all with the clapper of his bell. The Concubine did not seem the least bit nervous or shy. Cassius thought, well, I could be more than a creature, but he was still wary of a trick. She picked stones out of the packed clay floor and rhymed them. He presented her a birdwing fan. Side by side, their legs were a single description. I envy you, she said. Aging is merciless in my profession. The Leper was a young man. He was not surprised when she took down her beautiful hair and with it washed him up and down.

Effigies dangled from the highest turret. Cactus blocked the pantry entrance and garbage crammed the bake ovens full. Whelping went on under slogans written in candle smoke on the walls of the ransacked library, and the old desert men traded puppies. There was an intricate system of demerits. Turtle eggs appeared at every dungeon level. The nights got longer. Loyalties went untested. Life was cheap.

With grunts and bewilderment, the people massed to say contrition.

Rodolfo said go in peace.

THE DEEP BLUE
EASTERN SKY

●

O L I V I A from her bedroom window watched the honeyed light of October sunset move slowly up the street of brownstones to cast long shadows and soften contours. It turned leafless trees to mahogany, flared richly on the windows opposite, alluding to darkwood interiors, a warm sepia comfort of roast meat and carved furniture. Olivia brushed out her long, light-brown hair. Night fell and the city filled itself with rhetoric.

———

F R O M the parlor of the house on West Seneca Street in Buffalo she had looked out at junipers in silhouette like hearse plumes. There you always knew you were at the edge of wilderness. Factory soot came down with the snow. The immigrant shanties were just waiting for a match. Her father saw, practically, that he would never grow beyond the ceramic insulator business. He gave Olivia two years at Rose Hill College for Women, and then sent her to Aunt Catherine in New York.

"Make a good marriage," he advised. "Better yourself. Move up."

Aunt Catherine had twice married well, first to an importer of wines and spirits, and then to a delicate scion. Her widow's weeds were of the finest nankeen. She took her niece to the St. Regis for afternoon tea and was seated promptly. She showed how to use the mirror-lined entry of the Waldorf-Astoria's Palm Garden to maximum effect without at the same time being seen to loiter. Discretion meant, equally, that custard be concealed under leaves of pastry and that the string quartet perform behind a lacquered screen.

"The elegancies of life," Aunt Catherine explained, "when indulged to excess, cease to be elegant."

Restraint was the method of gentility. No matter that Catherine thirty years ago would squat at the edge of a trash fire to pull hot mickeys out and pass them, split and steaming, to her brothers: The distance traveled might tempt one to put on airs, but you resisted, you smoothed over, and that was precisely the point.

The upper levels of the city were vigilant, alert to every signal. Catherine's house, at its demure, almost reticent address west of Madison Avenue, was furnished modestly, for comfort rather than display. To maintain it required but one in service: Delia from County Cork, who had been with Mrs. Howe since 1896. Sometimes, when Mum entertained, Delia brought Rose, her sister, to assist, but it was never more than once a week, there were never more than eight at table, and the dishes were simple: consommé, poached fish, an apple tart. Catherine, in her choice of guests, did not favor those who were "interesting," who would "make an impression." She set her store in the even temperament, the conversational style that seldom surprised. After the meal there might be lotto or whist (but never charades) or someone might play the piano, Strauss, for example, perhaps Victor Herbert, and by ten o'clock at the latest, one had retired.

Olivia grew restless. Where were the young men, her introductions?

"It doesn't pay to be eager," Aunt Catherine admonished her niece. "Don't rush."

"Well, certainly, I wouldn't want to reflect ill on you."

Olivia sulked. She had expected something else. Restriction went with Buffalo, where the chophouses and oyster saloons were exclusively for men, where a woman with a cigarette disturbed the peace. But if New York society meant more dreary constraint—rules of speech and dress and deportment—then what difference did it make to have come?

———

S H E wrote in her diary: "I cannot please everyone, and so I shall please no one." Then she let the nib rest on the paper so it would make a bloom of ink. Delia brought supper on a tray, macaroni in broth and an unbuttered roll.

"I made it so mild," she explained, "as you're still feeling poorly."

"I'll go to bed presently, Delia. I shan't need you further."

With the precision of some kind of woodcraft, Olivia shredded the roll, watched the shreds swell with broth and turn gray. Then she covered the tray with the blue linen towel and placed it outside the door.

She wrote: "Were I to die tomorrow, there would hardly be a dozen words to say about my life. This might be sad, but not, I think, so terrible."

———

A U N T Catherine agreed that there was no breach of good conduct in attending unescorted the Cooper Union summer lecture series, held on Wednesday and Friday afternoons. Ladies of refinement gathered in the hall to learn, or at least to hear, about formal gardens or Chinese porcelain or the migration of butterflies, and Olivia could come to no harm in their covey. Only now she was faced with her artless inabilities, her deficient taste. Buffalo, of course, had ill served her formation, that rail-head city with its beer-pail taverns and bargemen's dance halls, its mills and waterworks and foundries, its pride in noise, raw power, machinery. Should she tell those fine ladies she saw twice a week that the Indian name of Lake Erie meant "Walk-in-the-Water"? That once, at the Pan-American Exposition, she had seen Elena Granelli sing an aria from *La Traviata?* Well, it was better to say nothing at all. It was better not to be quaint.

At the end of July, Dr. Mylon Weems gave a talk on his journey by camel from Damascus to Tabriz. Arriving late, Olivia took a seat in the back row next to a clean-shaven man who made rapid notes on a pad. He smiled everywhere—at the high ceiling, at his shorthand, at the loquacious Weems, at her. And then afterward, finding her under the lobby sky-light, he quite gracefully, by way of explaining his scribbles, presented his card.

WARD CHASE, ESQ.
Reporter & Columnist
for
TOWN TOPICS

"I'm afraid you came to the wrong place for an interesting story," she said.

"My job often calls for invention."

"I don't know your publication," she said. "Perhaps I shouldn't."

Chase liked her blush very much, and the way she twisted the black strap of her purse around her white fingers.

There he was the following Wednesday ("Lives of the Avignon Popes"), but only, he said, as a disinterested spectator. When on Friday there was a postponement, Olivia circled the block three times, only to feign having newly arrived when at last she found him on the wide granite steps, expectantly poised in the sun.

Chase said: "I see how you are disappointed, but it's such a lovely afternoon. Might I walk a little way with you? Perhaps to some café serving ice cream?"

The pavement felt like glass. Olivia could scarcely breathe.

But such drama, she discovered, did not have long to run. It was soon enough clear that Chase valued her innocence as a mentor, and not as a suitor.

"You interest me," he assured her. "You interest me no end."

She had never been flattered so before.

"In a thoughtful way. Usefully. As an equal, if you see."

Olivia brought her hands up onto the marble counter, which was cool and slick, and said she did not know what to say.

"Just let me open your eyes," he said. "It's what I do best."

And Olivia thought: If I hope seriously to attract a suitor, I first will need the guidance of a mentor.

She blushed again. "May I have another lemonade?"

Chase was a reporter. He made explicit the social dichotomy which Catherine but fussily implied—that between Sherry's on Fifth Avenue and Rector's on Broadway, between the carriage trade and the sporting crowd, between port and champagne, sole and lobster thermidor, reticence and ostentation, restraint and indulgence, careful decorum and opulent excess.

"What may be deplored cannot be ignored," he said. "The drawing rooms and clubs are obsolete."

They were riding in a hackney coach past Bustanoby's, the Tivoli Palace theater, Murray's Roman Gardens.

"The real, immense drama of this continent is just beginning now," he said. "And this is where you'll find the players, not in some complacent enclave of old money."

They passed the Broadway Follies, Heffernan's, the new Knickerbocker Hotel.

"Blue blood ebbs," he said, "and red blood rushes in."

———

T H E fragrance of pomander balls, of lilac and clove, clung to Olivia's nightdress. Avoiding the oval washstand mirror, she plaited her hair into one long braid. She thought of her mother, wasted with confusion, smelling of thirst. "Seclusion" was a word that went with the long blur of Buffalo winter. And poor mother, in her last season, would eat nothing but sliced raw potato with salt, chanting, "Tubers and roots, tubers and roots." Olivia arranged herself under the bedding, knees bent to the wall, elbows pressing in. She heard clanking in the street, mutters, a hurt cat. And then everything was so still it felt as if she could blow out the windowpanes.

———

I N September, with no more afternoon lectures to pretend, Olivia announced her enrollment in an evening sculpture class.

"I need to broaden myself," she said to Aunt Catherine. "Don't you agree?"

"Let me find you a private instructor."

"But this way I can be with other girls."

"Your father has placed you in my care, Olivia. I appreciate that trust, and so should you."

"But I'm fine, really I am."

"Let me suggest . . ."

"And I've had my twenty-first birthday."

Olivia finally was able to dine where before she had only had lunch. The lavish interiors came to life. The colonnades and satin hangings, the gilt panels depicting imperial Rome, the crystal chandeliers and polished oak made more than a background; they dictated terms, defined possibility. These things were meant to stimulate, rather than intimidate. It was an open field, instead of an enclosure. You did not have to choose your words; shyness was unnecessary. The audience had reached the stage and it was playtime.

She watched Kreutzer, the nickel king, swallow two dozen oysters from a beer stein while a Florodora Girl tickled his ear; she found out that Lady Eve Sidwich used lemon juice to make her hair blond, and the one was no more enlarged at this rate than the other was diminished.

"The human scale," Chase said, "can be played on a piano."

She learned to distinguish timbales from croustades, palmettes from mousselines on the hors d'oeuvre cart, and how to joke with Swiss waiters.

Chase said: "You see? There's nothing to it."

She saw boxers and magnates together, tunesmiths, philanthropists, ward heelers, dowagers, acrobats, rug dealers, French farce ingenues with their white arms bared—and the columnist Chase, collector of tidbits, knew all their names.

"I wish I were a painter," Olivia said.

"No, no. The photograph is here. Oils and canvas are obsolete."

She tasted sorrel bisque and terrapin steak and pheasant breast, all for the first time. Between each course there came sherbet in white, or in mint or berry pink. And overhead, across a ceiling painted as the deep blue Eastern sky, electric stars were twinkling.

Aunt Catherine Howe had been waiting for at least an hour. Her mouth was tense and white at the corners.

"A friend has reached me by telephone. I know where you have been."

Olivia groped, fell back on the sofa.

"No more lies," hissed her aunt.

Coal was banked in the grate, and the room suffused with gaseous orange light.

"I've done nothing ignoble." Olivia opened her hands. "Nothing malicious."

"It isn't the doing but the seeming." Aunt Catherine turned her back. "And your indecency is plain."

"But it's friendship. The best sort of friendship, really. He only wants to guide me. To show me how things work."

"All the time *I* spent on your instruction, and you haven't understood a thing. We share that blame together, I suppose."

The room was too warm, too closed. And Catherine, who in her angular and calculated way had once seemed beautiful, now was an outgrowth of shadows.

"You'll have to go back north, of course," she said.

"But why?"

"Because as anyone can see, my dear, it's just where you belong."

———

I N her dream, the parlor on Seneca Street was lined with purple velvet, and the lamp wicks were turned up all the way. The table was set for a supper party, and the guests all were millionaire dogs.

The elkhound said, "The pictures are more degrading than the dime novel because they represent real flesh and impart their low morality directly to the senses."

The schnauzer puffed his cigar. "All these nickelodeon merchants are Jews."

The "Mother" character, in fact wearing someone else's face, counted out pickles.

It did not seem important to know what the weather outside was like. The falls would still be making electricity and the parlor on West Seneca would go on smelling of kerosene.

Their guests were not up to part singing. And when they caught on to the fruit pyramid, that it was made of wax, they turned ugly.

Her dream was a globe, and revolving inside it, in black type on Western Union yellow tape, was a headline: LIFE AS PREY.

Olivia woke gradually, in stages. She folded one ear over, feeling its cold edge. She recognized dawn without opening her eyes. "Paling in the east" came so insistently into her head, like ticking, that she had to get up and get away.

She found Delia with her head tipped back against the pantry door, the sash of her wool plaid wrapper loose and brushing the floor. Delia said she couldn't sleep for worrying about Rose and this boy she had fallen for head over heels. A boy from the docks, a scoundrel. She watched Delia rinse the pot with hot water and then put into it three measures of black tea from the square tin. She watched the stream from the kettle, and steam rebounding out the mouth of the white pot. Fine cracks in the glaze made it like the rolled shell of a hard-boiled egg. The neck and the base of the pot were edged in blue. The handle curved nicely. Delia said that at home in the hard times they boiled burnt crusts. She took down cups and Delia poured. The cream was just on the turn; it spread out in tiny ropes. Delia drizzled treacle off a thin souvenir spoon.

She said: "My father needs me to come back. He can't seem to get by on his own."

Delia blew across her cup. Light had come up to the window, and there was fog.

She said: "It would be wrong to look on it as duty."

In the beading of the sideboard edge were hardened drops of varnish.

And she said: "The ties that bind."

SOUTH SEA
SENSATIONS

●

Dumas was fond of the Great
Northwest, white mist and dark
coniferous trees. He said it reminded him of the Apennines,
where in fact he had never been. Lady Elaine cautioned him
on his driving.

"If we die, we die together."

"That sounds lovely," she said. "But I'd like to be able to
sit straight through the corners."

Looking at him in his coconut straw hat, the black
preacher suit he said could go ten thousand miles without
showing dirt, she thought: I'll never leave, even if my heart
would change.

When he pulled in at a stand selling myrtlewood salad
bowls, it was to offer the kid advice on how to improve his
attraction. She disliked little Dumas habits (fancy jokes, too
much pomade on his hair), but what she liked about him had
size: that he was fair, never overused an advantage, didn't feed
on contempt for suckers and rubes. He was a gentleman. He
could charm a bird right out of its cage, as she must have told
him a thousand times.

They drove on with the windows open wide, and Lady Elaine with her head on his shoulder.

"What I fell in love with the very first minute was how you could waltz."

"You were a feather in my arms," said Dumas the gentleman, author of *Torture & Catholicism, Dispersion of the Races,* and *Babyface Nelson, The Intimate Story,* animal impressionist on barnyard novelty records by the Jelly Roll Morton band, impresario of indoor bicycle races in Newark, beef-eating contests in Houston, manager of beauty queens, importer of tropical birds.

At the Endicott Lunch outside Roseburg, they took a booth midway between the entrance and the kitchen. Dumas ate his ham and white beans quickly, without looking up. Lady Elaine, slightly carsick, had tea. Two whores came in looking for men from the pulp mill. They wore tight dresses, open-toed shoes, and appeared to need sleep.

"Ah, *les nymphes du pavé*," said Dumas warmly, and invited them to sit down.

Lady Elaine felt her clothes, and what was underneath them, being closely appraised.

"Business bad?" said Dumas.

"These slobs." The tall one smoothed her marcel. "They don't know up from down."

"Maybe they got religion too much," said the small one, wetting her finger and dipping it in the sugar bowl.

Dumas bought them chicken dinners, a wedge of custard pie for his dessert, and an ammonia Coke for his lady.

"To keep your spirits up," he punned.

The Tremaine was homey, neither the best nor the worst in town. The stationery, which Lady Elaine used for a letter to her sister in Banff, proclaimed, "A Hotel For All The People."

Moths stuttered inside the lampshade. A snowy sleigh-ride lithograph was puckered under glass and hung askew.

Dumas, in pajamas, read aloud the *Billboard* carny gossip. He rolled into bed, smelling of pipe smoke. "My babies," he said, kissing her talc-dusted breasts, then turned on his stomach and fell fast asleep.

Lady Elaine kept awake an hour or more thinking how those girls could be murdered on the road and never even see their twenties. She'd traveled at that same age, from rodeo to rodeo with her father's bullwhip act, couldn't have been safer, more innocent. But those two had no protection, nothing to stop some great big lumberjack from tearing . . . The little one with glassy eyes defenseless most of all.

———

C O M I N G very late to breakfast, Lady Elaine found Dumas in the lobby giving one of his numberless histories to a traveler in plumbing supplies.

"My father grew up the youngest of ten in an Ozark cabin with only hand-dipped candles for light. They slept two and three to a hammock. They ate turnips like fruit, and acorns and hickory nuts. Cod-liver oil was too dear, so Grandma dosed them all with bacon grease. They were stupid and dirty, but true as steel."

As he came to the part about Pop dying of pneumonia hours before his swearing-in at the state capitol, Lady Elaine made her interruption.

"Herbert, let's be on time for our appointment." And she took his hand with a kind of motherly insistence.

Wasn't it a lovely summer? Fliers and film cans stowed in the big Packard trunk, they were on tour with *South Sea*

Sensations, shot at Pismo Beach with a cast of Mexican apricot-pickers, bare-breasted women in tablecloth sarongs, the men in lipsticked war paint. Forty seconds of autopsy film, skillfully intercut, fulfilled the "BIZARRE & HORRIFYING RITES OF SACRIFICE." They prospered.

"Boobs and blood," Dumas said. "You can't beat it with a stick."

It was an ensemble operation, a labor of equal lovers from setup to payoff. In town offices, like Chief Scarper's small brown one, Dumas set out the terms and Lady Elaine tuned the atmosphere: Men wary of a fast shuffle from the Husband might be reassured at dealing with a family business, and men ready to be greased, but uneasy with women, might take comfort in the Wife's hard pug face and hoarse profanity.

"We've had stag films before. And nekkid girls, live ones," said Scarper. "But it weren't advertised."

"We present this as educational." Dumas swiped at a fly. "A documentary."

Scarper tapped his oily forehead. "You mean to put this on at the school or something? Kee-rist."

Dumas was patient. With his finger he guided the Chief's attention to the seventh and eighth lines of the flier:

NOT FOR THE SQUEAMISH OR FAINT!
MATURE ADULTS ONLY—PLEASE

"And what you got's gonna square up with this come-on?"

Dumas made a steeple of his hands. "Quoting from Eckermann's *Conversations with Goethe*, 'The papers were brought in, and we saw in the Berlin *Gazette* that whales had been introduced on the stage there.' Of course, upon investigation, this proved to be no more than a porpoise in heavy costume. Do you see my point?"

"I do not."

"My husband can be so abstruse at times." Lady Elaine smiled indulgently. "What he means is that people will see what they want to see. You just have to give them a chance."

"Five bucks a ducat, you say?"

"Anything less, they feel they won't have had their money's worth," answered the Husband. "And you get a buck off the top of each one."

Scarper raked his nails across the pilled green desk blotter. "Odd Fellows hall might be free. Lemme make a call."

———

N O O N had burned away morning damp. They made their way back to the Tremaine through lunchtime foot traffic, issuing fliers just now detailed, in bright red ink, by the Chief's personal secretary, with time and location.

"I don't like to see you spoil those beautiful eyes with squinting," Dumas said, guiding Lady Elaine into a pawnshop, where she could pick out a pair of dark glasses while he talked up the owner.

"Shalom. So how's by you?"

"These are a perfect match for my combs."

They left with blue lenses in tortoiseshell frames and a flier in Siegel's window.

Two blocks from the hotel, lolling on the stairs of a triple-decker wooden apartment house, there was that little whore. Lady Elaine, stern, gave over the revolver from her purse, first wiping it clean, and said, "Anyone tries to get rough, you shoot his dick off."

The girl buzzed her lips and spun the chamber.

———

S R O at $5 per. Seasonal aromas: drugstore whiskey, anxious flesh on varnished folding chairs. Noisemakers: brogans scuffing the pine floor, crackling newspapers fanned, coughs and snorts releasing tension of the attention Dumas commanded with—

". . . Are we repelled by their savagery? Charmed by their simplicity? What can we really know of these strange tribesmen and their isolated land of scoria and marl?"

—such spieling as Lady Elaine put into her negative division of fancy jokes. But she knew this was his instrument, and that to play fresh inventions each time meant more to him than money. She threaded the film through the projector, trued it in the gate.

". . . filling this hall in such numbers to be startled, astounded, astonished, seeking not the satisfaction of curiosity but stimulation for the heart and mind. And so, my friends, now shall you have it."

She lowered the phonograph arm and the Boswell Sisters sang "Down Among the Sheltering Palms." Gestures dappled the screen.

———

B E F O R E the astonishing film, it had been two-cent stamps sold through a classified ad: "Color portrait engraving of George Washington. Send your $2 now! P.O.B. 3G, Ansonia Station, N.Y."; before that Love Lockets peddled on amusement piers from Norfolk to Myrtle Beach to Mobile; before that a turf advisory service that once too often gaffed a dentist with connections. Dumas served not quite half of an eighteen-month sentence at Sing Sing. His cellmate, Monk Dershowitz, the Club Royale killer, knew interesting card tricks.

And some while before that, on the veranda of a Sarasota hotel overlooking the Gulf, Dumas and Lady Elaine had met for the first time. They were at separate tables with coffee and rolls and striated butter curls on ice. They wore white: his plus-fours and pullover, her silk blouse and aeronaut's jodhpurs.

At that time, to everyone but the natives, Florida was novel, exotic, a tropical backdrop even the dullest might play against, granting equally to Buick dealer and tycoon grounds for sport and a climate for folly. Banjo bands and coon dancers roamed Sarasota; the Asola Theater had been rebuilt out of constituent parts sent from Venice.

"May I join you?"

"I don't mind." She smiled while hiding her teeth.

Dumas looked past the hawk nose and into her deep-green eyes.

She was first to turn away. "You must be dressed for golf," she said. "It couldn't be a lovelier day."

"No, no. Billiards is my game."

She thought: He's not so much older than me. In his forties, or perhaps a bit more.

"I know what you mean," she said. "I've always been at my best indoors."

There was something like bergamot in her perfume. Dumas offered a cigarette. They lied readily to each other for several minutes.

"Would it be rude to order champagne at this hour?"

"I don't mind," she'd said.

———

"MARRY me." Dumas cut the salt air with the stiff white brim of his hat.

South of Coos Bay, still half a day from the California line, they'd stopped for razor clams and a game of miniature golf. Lady Elaine had just stroked the ball under a lighthouse —its wire form showing through cracks in light blue cement— round a banked turn, off a pipe rail at two sharp angles, and into the cup.

"You're such a ham," she said.

Lady Elaine wore her dark glasses. The bulb enclosed in the lighthouse blinked invisibly in direct sun.

"Have I ever once teased you with this in twelve years?"

"No, never. And don't spoil the record now."

"Now is late."

His shy sobriety frightened her.

"Shall I drive?"

"I mean in the game. Late in the game."

"Come on, you need a drink."

Dumas touched her face. "I mean it's something we should do before we get too tired. Before we get to where it won't matter." She looked out at the unreasonable tumbling of the sea. "Let's make for Nevada and you can think about it on the way."

"I already am. I'm remembering what it took to get free of my last husband."

Dumas reseated his hat. "Nobody but me will ask you, and I won't again."

"I don't mind."

Lady Elaine thought of the little whore. Down a road black with rain, unconsciously clicking the headlights from dim to bright to dim and back again, she felt her heart change.

DEVELOPMENT

●

L IGHT-HEADED from si-
lence, Brick stopped in Canyon
City to have the car monogrammed. A Sioux in watch cap and
coveralls appraised him as a surgeon might. Gesturing, they
arrived at a figure. The Sioux had piano player's hands.

Raptors floated on thermals that rose from the parking
lot. Brick, who deplored pathos, began to count in his head.
Observe geology. Check tire pressure. Take photos: distancing
factor. He bought pemmican and crackers from a vending
machine that beeped twelve bars of Gershwin, G. Cautiously
approaching the municipal beach, he saw it was deserted, and
crouched in the shade of styrene palm leaves to eat.

Monotony of the waves.

Gull talk.

What continued to bother him was that analog wiring, one
thing always leading to another: intricate rake trails in the
sand furnishing the notes for a Japanese temple courtyard. He
missed the clarity of no connections, of ignorance. And he
continued to suspect that someone else had control, that he was
being moved from panel to panel like a man in a comic strip.

How long and how far? How many stolen hotel towels?

Brick could not remember preparing for this trip, let alone on what day and in what city it had begun. He did remember waking up behind the wheel, having slept only for a second, then swerving past the reflective eyes of a large mammal, and over median grass. How much luck had that used up?

The white Gothic B's to right and left of the hood scoop were, Brick realized only now, wrong side round to his view. He checked the expressions of oncoming drivers, for whom it was right side up, but these were unreadable.

Well, he could adjust.

That was the idea of travel, anyway.

On the far outskirts of Ciudad Radiofonica, he pulled over for a girl with a sign charcoaled, "Pilgrimage to Family Crypt."

"How far you going?"

"Le Havre."

Close up, it was easy to see that the pigtails and pinafore were an affectation, that she was quite a bit older than she was trying to seem.

"Brick Bradford," he said, opening his hand. "Chemist, explorer, tight end."

"The name is Boots."

"And you're on a pilgrimage."

"Oh, that's just a gimmick," she said irritably. "I won this tour in an essay contest sponsored by the Optimists Club. I wrote 'Emergency Styling: A Sonata in Verbs.' But I discover some empty promises, like yesterday, this allegedly prepaid hotel, my room key won't go through the wax they've jammed in the lock, and I have to skip. Real hospitality. Am I talking too much?"

Hedgerows had given way to olive groves and low, dry-laid stone walls. Cattle egrets flew up out of a ditch. A boy led a gray donkey laden with firewood. The donkey's expression said: I am not here.

They stopped at a trattoria with outdoor tables and ordered clam salad. Bright plastic soft drink crates were stacked against the fence. Across the road, on the one remaining wall of a house destroyed by fire, posters for a ninja film had been pasted upside down.

Brick wiped his plate clean with bread. "Do you believe in coincidence?" he said.

"I never ask myself."

"How about destiny? Do you believe in destiny? That we're really not in charge?"

"I ignore that."

She spoke too slowly, too carefully, for these responses not to have been learned in advance.

"Is it true that sharks never sleep?" he said in the next panel, by way of experiment.

"Too obvious." She pushed out her lower lip.

"What color are my eyes?" he said, covering them with his hands.

"Too romantic," she said, taking her musette bag and slithering through the curtain of beads that hung in the doorway.

By the time Brick understood that she would not come back out, had ditched him via the back door, crickets were sounding, wild thyme aroma had vanished behind tour bus exhaust, and blue Xmas bulbs glowed along the roofline. His incoherent revenge was to run out on the check.

In the center of the right front seat, as if deliberately placed, and so demanding to be read, was a sheet of bond paper folded into an airplane:

Rex—

We never talk any more, really talk. You're so busy with your "graphs and charts." And whoever answers your phone there is not passing my messages along. Or possibly you are only pretending to be ignorant of them? It is humiliating for me to appear at canoe class alone. It is so painful for me now to remember our first summer at the cottage, you nursing my sunburn so tenderly. Last week at breakfast when I showed you my plane ticket, you laughed and laughed. Maybe you are laughing as you read this, I don't know. But if you miss me and are sorry, it is not too late. Write c/o Hotel Empire, El Kharga.

Optimistically,
B.

Once again, B.B. was subject to the caroms of association. Having snapped at the end of the second sentence that this was the letter to her husband that had never been sent, he thought of the extinct passenger pigeon, the Transatlantic Cable, and Riverdale High valentine cards after that, Lulu with her haughty, rhodium-plated poodle pin. All without any proof that he was remembering his own experiences, and not someone else's.

Heat lightning over the plains. Phone-talk radio. He couldn't keep his eye off the mileage counter, reassured by any movement of the numbers.

"Go ahead, Emporia, Kansas," said the phone-talk host.

White moths continued to collide with the windshield, spattering their essential liquors.

"I have a question for Major Hoople," said the voice from Emporia.

He placed another nicotine lozenge under his tongue.

The Dew Drop Inn concierge refused his check and mimicked his bad pronunciation. The kitchen was closed, she told him, and then called the bellhop to help ridicule his clothes.

"But this is what I always wear," Brick protested, flouncing his white linen suit, smoothing the lavender band of his boater.

The bellhop's little finger, which had lost its top joint, first touched the side of his nose, then traced his eyebrows.

"Clochard," he said. "Walking backwards around the world."

Brick had no choice. He dined under the sodium lamps of a roadside park that memorialized the Colorist Uprising of 1968. The cold forests around him were thick with fir and spruce. Raccoon dogs called to one another. He ate a bologna-and-sweet-relish sandwich. He tried to make a nest on the slippery back seat of the car, and everything came apart. Sleep came hard; it was like the finish line of a forced march. He shivered and twitched with a dream that went something like this:

Moving through a suite of apartments in a rose-pink building at the corner of Wilshire and Western. Eating jellied consommé at a glass table, taking Russian cigarettes from a Chinese box. Chrome accents. White bisque bas-relief Pegasus over the fireplace. Parrot climbing drapes. Santa Anita results on radio KNBC interrupted for bulletin flash. "Rex missing! Posse formed! Search dunes!"

Brick's descent from the mountains was one long afternoon of switchbacks. A light rain fell. The pastures were empty. Gasoline was unavailable in village after village, but wine was everywhere. Fog lay in the valley. Pennants dangled over the roadblock and militiamen in silver shirts searched every car for booty from last night's tomb rifling. They pried up mirrors and slashed water bags.

Now Brick recognized all plot elements as lab work, a run of testing obstacles, captive panels clocked and rasping with the stylus over an unspooling graph paper band. Fine, then. Over we go.

And there were promising dust clouds. Slag heaps and cactus signaled the final push. He mopped himself with a blue shirt, tied it over his head; and then, ominously, he ceased to sweat. Fear preceded caution: character was fate. He rolled the windows up as he neared the city. Men in white djellabas lined the road, and they were not too proud to beg.

The Hotel Empire lobby smelled of beeswax and mice. Bullet-riddled furniture had been pushed all into one corner. The hollow columns were wrapped in gold foil. Brick had no trouble locating his man, nibbling salt plums at a glass table beside the pool, sunlight glinting on his hair.

"Glad you could make it," Rex Morgan said.

"I guess I'm what you'd call kind of a stooge."

"You were allowed to find me. Not encouraged, not coerced."

"Fine. Just fine. How much luck does that use up?"

"I'm a doctor. I can give you new prints, a different face."

"What good would that do?"

Brick saw that his next line would be, "Where is the ethical component?" But he was able to stop himself. Suppose his words were like antibodies: formed in the past as specific response, then stored for use? He could learn to dissolve them.

"Our too shabby flesh, hmm?" Morgan said, pulling Brick's hand to his throat to feel the driving blood.

Dusk had already happened. Day, having moulted like

an insect, exuded a fresh night. Children crouched inside the sandstone wall to pee. Voices out of the lemon grove turned bitter. A salesmen of very first-rate Irish tweed inquired at the desk about licensing. Glasses of sweet mint tea were brought to the table. Morgan tilted in his chair to drink. His cheeks were rouged, his pupils unusually large.

"Is this too scenic?" he asked. "Just say the word."

"I have an awareness problem. It makes me a little jumpy."

"I'm a doctor. I can take care of that too."

"Drugs? A regimen?"

"I know, I know. That's no way to solve it." Morgan clenched his teeth, batted at a wasp, edged forward. He sighed. "Just look around you. It's everything that's wrong with development policy."

"A man, a plan, a canal, Panama." Brick's antibodies were hooked in and he could not interrupt the process. "Scenic, romantic, historic. Resources alarming in their potential, and the keystone for a vital future. Am I talking too much? Just say the word."

"You need to go up and rest," Morgan said palliatively. "The fighting won't begin for hours."

Fresh smell of citrus. Face of travel clock averted. Wallpaper with a repeating figure of minarets. More than a presence, dismay. Recognizable. As yellow fat taste in mouth. As harsh feel of sheets on skin. Possible tampering with chemistry? Question Rex, but he won't answer anymore. Room completely dark now. From here cannot quite see over wall. Impossible.

The moon was high, half full. Goats foraged in the empty riverbed. Scooters buzzed and wives bargained for rolls of toilet paper. A prerecorded muezzin's call was inadvertently set off. Tires burned in the street beside the monogrammed car.

ROSELLA,
IN STAGES

●

[6]

Some guests on the porch had just returned from a hike to the falls. They were loud. Rosella, crouching, studied them from inside the hemlock hedge. One fancy lady had little moss bits on her shoes.

"What swells the heart is timelessness."

"I must disagree. Rather, it is purity in the here and now."

This city man wore clothes like a farmer would, and went out every morning to draw. Rosella had followed him to Ship Rock and seen him pee over the edge. And then right away after, Mama looked at her outside the kitchen, said, "Have you been eating pitch again, Rosella?" and smacked her hard.

Mama didn't like so many guests this time of year, and having to cook for them all because Minnie was away with hectic fever. The foreign people wanted trout for breakfast every day. Which Poppa said meant they weren't Jews, at least.

Getting out of the hedge meant torn stockings, so Rosella

went in the barn to take them off. It was nice to kiss the horse. He gave back warm air out of big nostril holes and pushed with his head. Rosella buried her stockings and shoes in the oat bin. She would say a man from the woods had robbed her.

They were still loud on the porch. About the President's doctors in Buffalo saying he ought to pull through.

"No reason for a one of these anarchists to be on the loose."

"But how to discover each one? They are the most devious people."

"Czolgosz? Anyone with two z's in his name, lock him up."

Rosella picked up an interesting stone.

[19]

The cylinder slowed on the Edison machine, and Rosella turned the handle so they might hear the rest of "Jitney Elopement" at its proper speed. Caroline halved the distance between them on the divan and proffered on her snow-white hand a nugget of crystallized ginger.

"I am quite sure," said she, "that I have never had a more enjoyable Christmas."

All the guests but her had retired. Beech logs popped and settled in the fireplace.

Caroline looked searchingly at Rosella. "And I hope it is not out of my place to say how glad I am that what between us began as an agreeable acquaintance has, in these few days, grown into a warm, close friendship."

The song had ended, but Rosella, in flushed perplexity, did not lift the needle.

"It seems so sad to me that circumstances by morning must force us apart." Caroline's green eyes glistened in the flickering light. "Might I beg you now for one goodbye kiss as a token?"

Rosella stiffened when the tip of Caroline's tongue grazed her lips. She smelled ginger and melting wax.

"Oh, my darling," Caroline wailed, pulling desperately at the fastenings of her bodice. "I would face eternity for you."

[32]

After Sunday Mass they left the girls with Otto's mother and drove on out to where the hotel had been. It was a cool day, but clear, and the leaves were still green. They teased and held hands in the car until the road curled away from the water and steepened.

Daylilies had gone wild all over the char. Foundation lines were untraceable by eye.

"This was the dining hall," said Rosella, standing in burdock up to her knees.

Otto had a piece of melted glass, twisting it in his big knobbed hand like a pitcher feeling the seams of a baseball.

"You had to balance plates all the way up your arm," said Rosella.

Hair falling over her eyes was lank and wanted washing, the way everything wanted it—roasting pan, black skillet, walls and windows, the children when they filled their diapers, Otto when he came off a train: the day run to Albany, the two-day run to Utica.

"And the flagpole was here," she said, looking across the gorge for those very private silver-birch cabins called Elka Park.

Otto lifted the back of her plaid skirt. "You smell like ferns, like you was ten years old."

Crows could be heard, but not seen.

"Feel good you married me?" (He meant, "Wouldn't you rather have the hotel?")

"Mostly."

"Mostly? What the hell is that?"

"Only don't ask that way," said Rosella in a voice that was harder than she wanted it to be. "Say, 'Do you love me?' and it's nothing but yes."

Otto sulked step-by-step to the car. Rosella opened her hand on gleaned hemlock cones and went after him.

[45]

Liddy drew her thumb along the chromed edge of the sideboard. She decided to smile.

"Mom, I'm going ahead whatever you say, so why don't you say yes and make it nice for both of us."

Rosella couldn't decide anything. She pushed her glasses up and rubbed the sides of her nose. A truck passed, then another.

"This house is too close to the road," she said.

Liddy played exasperation, tsking and rolling her eyes. "Why can't you see what an important opportunity this is for a girl my age? Gosh sake, Mom, do I want to spend my whole life darning socks and pickling beets and all that? Do I?"

Rosella took no offense. She leafed through the paper. A comedy with Joel McCrea was playing.

"Because I'm calling Merle right now and telling her to get the tickets. I mean it."

Rosella thought of how long it had been since Otto had written. Maybe his freighter was in a port he couldn't spell. But she had Prince Valiant, Helen Trent, her chickens and roses to fuss with. Was that why she didn't miss him more?

Liddy dialed six numbers, hung up, and came clattering back.

"You need quieter shoes," her mother said.

"We need you to lend us the money."

Liddy was going to cry.

[67]

There were the same two chickadees that came every day to the feeder.

She said, "Otto, does it hurt bad today?"

He blinked, smiled at the falling snow.

The man on television said, "Tell her what she's won, Johnny."

There was the magazine without pictures which Liddy had sent because it printed her article: "Kings of Song: Armenian Bards in the Seventeenth Century." She picked it up to try to read it again, but the language was thick. Bard? Someplace they had a dictionary, but it meant climbing upstairs. She wondered how Liddy could be a professor of music and not play any instrument.

It was going to be dark early. She noticed surfaces where snow caught: in a line on the back of the iron deer, where the gnome folded his arms and on parts of his cap. John Ostrander drove a sand truck up the road. Probably John. She couldn't see into the cab.

The college was in Oregon, but Liddy called each week, took an interest. Still, the big place in her heart belonged to Carol, with a husband in jail and sloppy kids and running out most nights. She knew this was "wrong," but some things were just there and you didn't decide.

Otto teased her by slurping his tea. He made waggish eyes.

The man on television said: "See you next time."

[85]

Girl abusing my arms for the ivy bottles, loud, hair shiny.
Married to Jesus and wearing white to show that off, no need so
loud and cheerful then try to give pills like the sacrament.
Change the rules once you learn following, new tricks for the
dog, and marrying Otto in beige, pure as I could be, Mama
angry about all the sewing, always true to that, hands on hips,
middle of that fire probably, giving hell and hail Columbia.
Otto never pretended, fell in love with the way he died and
left before hot afternoon dill cucumber soup and white stone-
ware bowls in all hands on deck for their day not his to wake
up on stage, costume faces and white glove pressing—Anita
and a black fan   three Wolvens   Ed and Norma   TC
who punched him in the railyard   confused Connie   Fratello
who bought the meatmarket   Ethel and Sid   the fat Garside
kids   Shorty and Moira who flew   a woman from Ker-
honkson with dirty boots   and hid inside the hedge me
seeing them all.